THE BLACKBIRD
SINGULARITY

MATT
WILVEN

Legend Press Ltd, 175-185 Gray's Inn Road, London, WC1X 8UE
info@legend-paperbooks.co.uk | www.legendpress.co.uk

Contents © Matt Wilven 2016
The right of the above author to be identified as the author of this work has
been asserted in accordance with the Copyright, Designs and Patents Act
1988. British Library Cataloguing in Publication Data available.

Print ISBN 978-1-7850796-8-9
Ebook ISBN 978-1-7850796-9-6
Set in Times. Printed in the United Kingdom by Clays Ltd.
Cover design by Simon Levy www.simonlevyassociates.co.uk

Matt Wilven was born in Blackpool in 1982. After receiving an MA with Distinction in Creative Writing, he spent the next ten years moving around, working jobs and honing his craft. *The Blackbird Singularity* is his debut novel. He lives and writes in London.

Visit Matt at
mattwilven.com
or on Twitter
@mattwilven

For Saskia

FOREWORD
FROM DR ELEANOR LONGDEN

"Madness," says Shakespeare, "must not unwatch'd go." And certainly, for those of us who experience a serious breakdown, there is a level of spectating and scrutiny. Society stares at us, science dissects us, our lives fall apart, and we are forced to watch it happen. When I was eighteen, I went mad. It occurred in a sputtering cauldron of trauma, loss, injustice and despair, and for many years I simply gave up hope and surrendered to the loss of myself and the life I'd been supposed to have. *Gone mad* people sometimes say, as if madness is a discrete destination or place, and this is also true. Such extremes of suffering are a journey which we often need to make, and are forced to travel alone. Maddened, then, yes — driven mad. But not ill. To me, the term "illness" privileges biology. It's suggestive of random aberrance, an arbitrary, catastrophic misfiring of neurons. I believe very strongly that what happened to me was not a piece of biological bad luck. Rather, it was a sane and understandable response to deeply insane and abnormal circumstances. A narrative not based in disease and disability but in meaningful distress and a struggle for survival. In the years since, this has been the emphasis of my professional career: that what gets labelled mental illness is in fact an intelligible, ordinary reaction to incomprehensible and extraordinary pain, and that the therapeutic response demands we bear witness to the person's story. Not "*what's wrong with you?*" but rather "*what's happened to you?*"

The Blackbird Singularity charts the journey of someone driven slowly, exquisitely, excruciatingly mad by the weight of his own anguish and unresolved grief. In discontinuing his medication, Vince is forced to confront the unspoken and unspeakable. It is a voyage that is both catastrophic and liberating: beautiful and tortured in turns. As readers, we witness the visceral complexities of a man being undone and remade as he attempts to engage with a past he believed to be buried; yet which is ultimately proved to be buried alive and desperately demanding acknowledgement. There are considerable risks in abruptly withdrawing from psychiatric drugs, and *The Blackbird Singularity* deals honestly and unflinchingly with these. Vince's struggles are not romanticised or sanitised: we are never in any doubt of his desolation; never unaware that this is a man clawing together every possible resource – mind, body, soul – to fight for his life. The novel explores some profound issues: what does it mean to be mad? To be sane? Who makes that judgement, and how permeable are the boundaries of reason and rationality anyway? How can creativity, imagination and invention complement positivism and logic? As such the book can be enjoyed on several levels – a puzzle box of questions with no easy answers – and all handled by Matt Wilven with considerable deftness, wit, wisdom and compassion.

Any novel, and particularly a first novel, that can engage with mental health issues in such an engaging and intelligent way is to be warmly recommended. But one does not need personal experience of emotional distress to appreciate the nuances and pleasures of a good story, well-told. If you have known what it is to love, to lose, to persevere, to laugh with friends and sigh with family, then you will find something that resounds with you within *The Blackbird Singularity*.

My own personal resonance I would like to share here. It was several years ago, and I was sat on a bench overlooking London's Parliament Hill with my then-partner as I told him more details than I ever had before about my life. It was a story in several acts: trauma, degradation, madness, redemption. Of suffering, sadness and senseless loss; but also of hope, healing and transformation. I disclosed the years of abuse that had driven me mad in the first place, the pessimism and pathology that came after, the schizophrenia diagnosis, and – finally – the freedom that came from reinterpreting my distress as something meaningful to be understood, explored and acknowledged. It took a long time, and when I looked over I could see tears in his eyes.

"Someone died in that place," I said quietly, although I didn't really know what "place" I was referring to. Somewhere ineffable, I suppose; that dark, wretched wasteland called The Past.

"I suppose someone did," he replied, and there was pause. "But you know, someone else was saved."

On the way to the Tube station, we stopped for a drink. The pub was playing a Beatles medley, and I remember "Blackbird" beginning as we took our seats. One of the lyrics had a curious relevance: the reminder that even if one's wings have been broken, it's always possible to learn to fly again.

Eleanor Longden, PhD's TED talk, *Learning From the Voices in My Head*, was featured on the front page of the *Huffington Post* and has been named by the *Guardian* newspaper as one of "the 20 online talks that could change your life". It has been viewed over 3 million times and translated into 36 languages.

FIRST
TRIMESTER

ONE

An event horizon is a mathematically defined boundary around a black hole. It is the point from which light can no longer escape the pull of the centre and all possible paths lead further into the hole. Beyond it, gravity is thought to be so powerful that it stretches and tears matter into subatomic strings. Outside, observers see it as a black surface upon which things darken and disappear. They can use the boundary to calculate a few simple facts – such as mass, spin and charge – but they can only theorise about what happens in the space beyond it.

Lyd leaves the house for work around 7:30am. I'd been listening for the sound of her shower to stop but drifted off. I sit up and rub my face, annoyed about missing her. Lithium doesn't discriminate between the important and unimportant moments in life. My mornings are always fuzzy.

After using the toilet I look at myself in the bathroom mirror. The tired man behind the glass has aged a lot in the last two years. His black hair is mottled grey at the temples. The skin around his eyes is dark, bruised almost, but not on the surface; the beating has come from the inside. There is a discrepancy between the perceived morbidity of his character (someone in his late fifties) and the age of his physical body (somewhere in its mid-thirties) but his end is definitely closer than his beginning.

Downstairs, I make myself a coffee and a couple of slices of toast and listen to a John Lee Hooker compilation. The phone starts ringing after my first bite. I leave the music on and continue eating, letting it ring out. Lyd's left half an old packet of sultanas on the kitchen counter with a yellow Post-It note stuck to the front. It reads: *For the birds*. It's impossible to fault her pragmatism, thinking about feeding the neighbourhood birds minutes after seeing me sleeping through one of the definitive moments in our relationship.

I open the pack and smell them. They look sticky and are beginning to ferment so I open the sliding door and dump them on the frosty lawn. The majority fall out in one big clump and break into three pieces when they hit the hard earth. It's too cold to bother scattering them properly.

I slide the patio door shut, pull a chair away from the kitchen table, wrap my hands around my cup of coffee and watch the white lawn. Within seconds a blackbird arrives, and then another. Soon there are nearly a dozen of them fluttering about, raising tiny clouds of hoar frost and trying to win a few moments on top of one of the sultana clumps. I'm not sure how long I sit watching them but, for the first time in a long time, I experience the creative glimmer of a new idea.

After a couple of minutes the idea is outshining my interest in the birds so I venture upstairs to my writing desk. Words flow out of me all morning. There's no double-checking my email, no scrolling through news sites or vacantly gazing at lists of jobs. I don't even turn my computer on. I just sit down and write in my notebook for four hours.

Around lunchtime the broken images of the story stop appearing in my head and the words clog up. I realise that I've forgotten to take my lithium. I consider taking it now but what I just wrote felt like a breakthrough. I want to keep hold of this clarity of mind. I bite the inside of my right cheek and decide not to take it. I go out for a twenty-minute jog instead.

After a shower and some lunch I head back to my writing room. I stop at Charlie's bedroom door. It's been over six months since I've faced it, and Lyd doesn't like it when I go in, but I feel like I have to. My hand trembles as I reach for the knob. I wonder if I'm already withdrawing from my medication or if I'm genuinely afraid.

The room is exactly the same – off-white wallpaper with pleasant childhood objects dispersed like polka dots, planetary-themed carpet, *Toy Story* bedcovers, wardrobe cluttered with cartoon stickers and scribbled crayon drawings, plastic whiteboard with a picture of our family drawn in stick man form, a cheap wooden trunk too small for all the toys – typical stuff for a four-year-old raised in a London suburb. The only unique thing is the low-hanging moon I made for him in one of our make-believe sessions. I push it with the tip of my toe and watch it sway back and forth.

His favourite soft toy lies by the pillow on the bed. He was probably the last person to touch it so I don't want to disturb its position. It always looked like a limp, dead ferret, even when it was new, and we could never get it away from him. Where did it even come from? I look around and find myself sighing. The sound that comes out contains an unintended groan.

I pick up a retro 1960s robot from the windowsill; a toy we bought as an ornament. It's red, quite heavy and shaped like a squat cone. Its mouth is a chrome grill and the eyes are blue sirens. There is nostalgia in its naïvety, cuteness based on the fact that the original creator had been unable to form a clearer vision of the technological future. My jittery hands fumble and drop it.

The robot is motionless on the floor, part of the wrong future. I scowl at it, hate it, and find myself stamping on it three times. It doesn't break. It's surprisingly sturdy. The pounding hurts my foot through my shoe. Grimly amused by my failure to destroy it, I pick it up and put it back in the same position on the windowsill. My hands are steady again.

I begin to feel like I'm loitering so I leave the room and go back to my writing. I find myself working on another new story. It's set in a completely different time and place but it belongs in the same universe as the one I was writing this morning. I don't know how or why I know this. I just know that I feel alive in a way that seems forgotten. I'm focused and productive. Time is moving so fast that I almost can't believe it when I hear Lyd's key in the front door.

When people ask Lyd what she does for a living she usually answers with something self-deprecating like, "Sums." Sometimes, when pushed, she says, "I'm a physicist." Until four years ago she was an unsung hero in the world of particle physics and a some-time lecturer at Imperial College London. Then her book *Mini-Novas: The End of Science or the End of the World?* became a crossover hit (her publishers forced the subtitle – it upset Lyd for weeks but also ensured that she sold a lot of books). It's about the role of particle accelerators in the future of science and, specifically, the potentiality of mini black holes. Now she occasionally does interviews on the news when they need someone to balance out a regressive or scaremongering perspective. She used to work much longer hours but a mixture of success and grief has put her in a position to choose her own working pattern.

I rush downstairs to meet her at the door. She looks tired but her mood lifts slightly when she sees that I'm smiling. I pick her up off the ground with a hug. Outside's chill covers her.

"Wait," she protests. "Let me get my coat off."

I put her down.

"Hello, lovely."

"Hello?" she says, curious. "What's up? You seem pretty buzzed."

"It's just good to see you."

"*Okay.*"

"I'm sorry I fell back to sleep this morning."

"It's fine," she says, hanging up her coat and grabbing her leather satchel back up off the floor. "What've you been up to?"

She walks through to the kitchen, dumping her things on the counter.

"Writing. A new thing. A couple of new things actually. They might be part of the same thing. I don't know yet."

"Oh? That's good."

"The first taste is always the sweetest."

"Great. Angela's going to be happy."

(Angela's my agent.)

She kisses me, a peck.

"How was your day?" I ask.

"Dull. Busy. Mostly dull. I think the problem I'm working on might be impossible. And pointless. Impossibly pointless."

"In the simplest terms?"

"Diffeomorphism covariance."

"Should I pretend to—"

"No. It's fine."

"Prawn stir-fry sound good?"

"Later." She pulls an opened bottle of white wine from the fridge. "I've got a headache."

I accidentally lower the right side of my mouth as she pours out a glass.

"What?" she asks. "One won't hurt."

"No. One's fine."

I can tell from her slightly aggressive manner that she doesn't want to talk so I go back up to my writing room for an hour. After a quiet dinner we watch a couple of episodes of a political drama that we've been hooked on for the last few weeks. I can't follow the story because our silence feels like the most prominent thing in the room. I rest my hand on her thigh. I kiss the side of her face. She doesn't turn to me once.

Around 10pm we go up to read in bed but I can't focus on my book either. I pretend to leaf through the pages for a few minutes and then put my bookmark back where it was when I started. Once she's finished her chapter she turns her bedside light off and lies with her back to me. I turn my light off and nestle up behind her. When I put my arm over her she rests her hand in mine but doesn't say a word.

It's 10:56am. I've slept in. I can feel the lithium depleting in me. It took me hours to get to sleep last night. I feel sluggish and depressed. I must have turned my alarm off and gone back to sleep but I have no recollection of doing it. Lyd's long gone.

I put some coffee on, pour myself a bowl of cereal and stand looking out into the back garden. One of the blackbirds is back. He keeps searching the grass and then jumping up onto our birdbath, turning his head sideways and, seemingly, staring at me in the house. He is more slight and agile than the typical adult male and moves quicker, with more poise and grace. I like the look of him.

After a couple of renditions of this lawn-and-birdbath routine I realise that he isn't searching the grass for bugs or food, he's pretending to. It's a show. He's begging, but not in a desperate fashion. He's like a busker or an entertainer. He doesn't want to work for a living, he wants to sing for his supper.

Intrigued as to whether I'm truly being manipulated by a blackbird (and amused enough to participate), I open a new pack of sultanas and throw out a handful for him. After cautiously flying up onto the garden fence when I slide the patio door open he quickly flies back down onto the lawn and hops from one sultana to the next, pecking and swallowing them. When he's done, before he flies away, he makes an oddly distinctive chirping sound:

– *chink-chink, chook-chook, chink-chink, chook-chook* –

The experience of watching him and being tweeted at cleanses my mind in some unfathomable way. The phased-out feeling I woke with dissipates. I close the sliding door, put my bowl in the sink, pour myself a black coffee and take it upstairs, ready to start writing.

It's already later than when I usually take my lithium and what I wrote yesterday felt so clear and concise. Right now, I need that clarity. The light fuzz of lithium can be a gift, it keeps me level, but when I'm trying to use my mind as a quick, sharpened tool it slows me down.

I spend all afternoon typing up and editing my work from the previous day. I cut all the abstract language and useless similes then eke out the right grammar and piece it into something more structured and interesting. Once it's in a readable state I go out for a jog.

I'm still in the shower when Lyd gets home from work. I can hear her on the telephone whilst I'm getting dressed. From her tone of voice and the cadence of her laughter (scathingly ironic but innocent of malice) I immediately narrow the person on the other end of the line down to her sister, Jayne, or her friend Gloria. I head downstairs.

"Yeah, he's here now... No. How could he? He never leaves the house. Ha, ha... Let me look at him... Yeah, he seems to be on pretty good form... Okay, I will... Okay. Bye, love."

She hangs up.

"I'll have you know I've been out running," I say, "today and yesterday. Was that Jayne?"

"Gloria," she replies, quickly descending from a world of open and carefree friendship into a more stressed and evasive mood.

"Did you tell her?"

"Tell her what?"

"About the pregnancy."

"No. Jesus, Vince."

"Sorry. How is she?"

"She says hi. She's good. Sergio's being a dick though."

"Oh?"

"He's hounding her. Asking who every text's from and if everyone in the office wears clothes like she does. I thought he was better than that."

"Come on, Serge is a good guy."

(Me and Sergio were friends before her and Gloria but now they meet up more than we do.)

"He's acting like an ape."

"She has changed though. She used to wear all those dark jumpers, loose trousers, everything covered up. They've been married eight years and she's suddenly started dressing provocatively. What's he going to think?"

"She can dress however she wants," says Lyd. "It's good that's she's coming out of herself."

"I didn't say she couldn't, or shouldn't, just that—"

"If Sergio can't deal with the fact that his wife wants to feel good about the way she looks—"

"It's not that. I think he just—"

She sees that I'm flustered by her aggression and restrains herself.

"We said we wouldn't do this," she says, smiling, changing tack. "And she does seem a little bit *too* relaxed lately, doesn't she? I wonder if she'd tell me if she was sleeping with somebody else. Sometimes you just can't tell. Who really knows anybody?"

"What if there were no rhetorical questions?" I quip.

Lyd rolls her eyes.

"So, good day?" she asks, insinuating that I'm chirpy again.

"I'm getting a lot out of these new ideas I'm working on. But I'm not really ready to talk about them yet."

"Still in the delicate stages?"

"Yes, like you," I say, moving in to hold her.

She tries to turn her head away from me.

"Hey," I protest, gently moving her face back towards me. "We've got to talk about it at some point."

"Not yet."

"After dinner?"

"Maybe."

"Definitely?"

"Maybe," she repeats, slipping out of my arms and grabbing some of her things to take upstairs.

"Do I not even get a kiss?"

She comes back and petulantly kisses me on the cheek. It's supposed to be funny but I watch her disappear with concern. Her wit is an act that has no joy in it.

I take my time making dinner to give Lyd some space. I cook an onion paste and a curry paste. I roast lots of sweet root vegetables in olive oil and seasoning. I mix them all together and add lots of tomatoes and cream. Then it's just a matter of waiting for it all to simmer down whilst I put the rice on.

Lyd loves curry and comes into the kitchen inhaling the aroma with her eyes closed.

"Smells delicious," she says, approaching the fridge and taking out a quarter-full bottle of white wine.

"Five–ten minutes," I say, adding some cloves and coconut milk to the rice and quickly checking to see if she's pouring out the whole quarter-bottle.

She is.

"What?" she asks, spotting my glance.

"Nothing."

I open the crockery cupboard and begin setting the kitchen table. Lyd helps and then takes her large glass of wine over and sits down.

"You know," she says, "my mum smoked twenty a day back when I was a bunch of mushy cells."

"And you blame her for having a small lung capacity whenever you get the chance."

I give the curry a stir.

"I'd have found another axe to grind." She takes a sip with a smile. "She knows I love her."

"I can never imagine your mum smoking... So, it's sinking in a bit?"

She looks at me blankly.

"The mushy cells?"

21

"A bit," she sighs, looking away from me, towards the steamed-up glass of the sliding doors.

I test the rice, there's still a tiny bit of crunch.

"We're going to have to talk about Charlie's room," I say.

Lyd skips a couple of beats before replying.

"No. We're not."

I turn to her.

"No?"

"There's plenty of other things to talk about first."

"True," I concede.

"It's early days."

"I know."

"You're always off in the future."

"I'm just trying to make sure we're ready for what's coming."

"Like I said, it's still early days. Try not to get carried away."

"Okay. But don't start using caution as an excuse not to talk about it."

"I'm not."

"I hope not."

I drain the rice in a colander and begin dishing out our food. I've made enough for four or five. It will serve us twice so I get some plastic boxes out and put the surplus in them.

"Are you okay, honey?" asks Lyd. "You seem very... lucid."

"Me? I'm fine."

I nod, perhaps a little bit too enthusiastically. Lyd tilts her head slightly.

"Okay."

We don't talk much over dinner. The curry has taken a while to cook so we're both hungry. We barely look up from our plates. Once we're done, Lyd says that she's tired. She can't seem to shift her headache from yesterday. I can leave the pots and pans. She'll do them in the morning.

I stay downstairs and do the washing up anyway. Cooking, cleaning, tidying up; I don't mind doing chores. I find them calming. And since Lyd is the only one earning any real money at the moment, doing most of the housework seems fair enough.

Drying my hands on a tea towel, I notice that they're trembling again. I grip and release the tea towel three times, slowly and firmly. I'll have to be careful Lyd doesn't notice these tremors. My promise to keep taking lithium is an important part of our relationship but my gut is telling me to stop. I have to stay sharp, get back in touch with myself.

I lie on the couch in the living room, staring at the ceiling. My mind wanders back to Charlie in the hospital, the day of his death. Astrocytomas are devouring his brain and spinal cord. We're entrenched in the stress cycle of his procedures: CT scan, MRI scan, biopsy, surgery, radiotherapy. We're hardly sleeping and rarely going home. Charlie has been having fits, losing his hair, vomiting in his sleep. It's beginning to seem like the hospital is trying to kill him, not save him. It's an institution of torture.

We've been living on the precipice of his death but when we're warned that today might be the day it seems like we haven't had a chance to prepare. There has to be something we should be doing, something we haven't thought of yet.

We sit on either side of him, both hold a hand and wait for the cancer to eat that final cell which will turn out his light. It takes sixteen hours. He's unconscious but makes soft, intermittent whimpers. When the sound of his flatline finally comes it tips all of my darkness out into the world. At first, Lyd thinks I'm crying but it's laughter, manic laughter so deep that it's silent.

Months earlier I asked one of the doctors why it's called *astro*cytoma. He told me it's because the cancer eats star-shaped brain cells. After this I started thinking of Charlie's brain as a universe plagued by a tiny black hole, swallowing all his stars. He started with a billion, you could see them in his eyes, and the cancer ate them up one by one until there were almost no stars left.

In the instant that I hear the flatline I imagine that Charlie's universe is the actual universe and that our sun, the last of the stars, has just been devoured. Everything is submerged in total blackness, the world is falling off its orbit, the moon is crashing into the Pacific Ocean, violent black winds are throwing clouds of people and cars and trees across countries and continents. Within moments there will be only chaos and death.

All this in a second.

Then I realise that the black universe where everything is about to die is not Charlie's, it's mine. This is the joke, where the laughter starts. It's the irony of not being connected to my emotional self. My feelings are in a dream universe. My actual body is relieved, happy, escalating towards euphoria. I'm divided in two. Reality's a trick. It's all one big joke.

After the laughter everything turns white. Credit card receipts tell a story of three manic days where I manage to spend much more than our life savings on hundreds of powerful torches and expensive lighting devices. At some point I crash our car. I vaguely remember telling everyone I meet that the night sky is a memory, that the stars are already dead, the light's about to end, we all need torches.

My delusions spike in a dark police holding cell where I keep demanding, in a shrill, loud voice, that the universe turn the sun back on. But every time I shout *sun* I start having these visual flashes of Charlie, dead in his hospital bed. Eventually, I figure out what's going on and have a fit of despair. They send me to a psychiatric ward.

After a couple of weeks of deep, silent grief, I start seeing the hoops they are holding up so I begin jumping through them. After another couple of weeks they diagnose me with stress-induced bi-polar disorder. Apparently, it's a relatively common way of not dealing with problems properly.

They prescribe a lifetime of lithium. It makes me feel confused and fuzzy so I intend to shrug it off once I get out but Lyd says that she won't take me back unless I promise to stay medicated. She is weak and barely able to talk but her relative resilience and strength fill me with inadequacy and shame. She has dealt with our son's funeral on her own whilst I was out there ruining what was left of our lives. I can't believe that anyone could have the depth of character to forgive me, but she does.

This was almost two years ago.

When I asked her why she had taken me back she answered:

"You loved him so much that you lost your mind."

I'm still on the couch when I wake up. It's morning, already light outside. There's a yellow Post-It note on my forehead: *If you're an idiot, read this*. I produce an almost non-existent snigger and sit up. My bodyweight is heavier than usual. I feel woozy and morbid.

Lyd's laptop is on the coffee table. I look up *lithium withdrawal* on the Internet and find that the only real side effect is a fifty-fifty chance of relapsing into mania. This dark gravity inside of me is all my own. My hands should *stop* trembling, not start, yet they tremble as I type. I clear the search history and go into the kitchen for some apple juice.

Outside, in the back garden, the blackbird from the day before is back and when he sees me through the window he starts doing his lawn-and-birdbath routine. I grab the bag of sultanas from the cupboard and open the sliding door. He flies up onto the fence. It's a chilly morning but, since I've woken up fully clothed and full of heavy shadows, I decide to take my apple juice outside and sit on one of the patio chairs. The blackbird watches me warily. When I throw a handful of sultanas onto the lawn he chirps up into the air:

– *choo-chin-chink-chica-chin-chink* –

After a few moments of anticipation he flies down and starts eating. It seems his call went out to his friends because, one by one, five more blackbirds fly down onto the lawn and begin eating the sultanas with him. As each bird arrives, the joy in me increases. I feel the sort of vacant serenity that I used to feel when I watched Charlie playing with his toys, unnoticed from his doorway. I'm looking in on a secret world. I've had a big hand in creating it but I'll never be able to truly join in or fully understand it.

Tensing all of my muscles against the bite in the air, I keep feeding them. Every time I throw more sultanas they all panic and fly up onto the fence and then, one by one, make their way back down onto the grass; always my little friend first.

After ten or twenty minutes, my feet go numb and my fingers turn blue but I feel inspired and capable and I'm wondering if the blackbirds have anything to do with my newfound creativity. I go up to my office and lose myself in yet another new story. Words fall through my pen with ease. I'm picking all the right details. The momentum is electric. Writing hasn't given me this much pleasure in years. I get into it so deeply that when Lyd comes home I'm still unshowered and in yesterday's clothes.

I go downstairs sheepishly to say hello. She's standing in the dark behind the front door in her long beige raincoat, holding her briefcase and handbag, eerily still.

"Lyd? *Lyd*?"

She drops her things, falls to her knees and hunches over.

"What's going on?" I ask, rushing over to her.

"I can't do it," she whimpers.

I stroke the back of her head and sit down next to her in the dark hallway.

"Talk to me," I say.

She's silent.

I rub her head so she knows that she's the centre of my thoughts. I prompt her to speak a few times but she either ignores me or repeats, "I can't do it." When she eventually sits up, she wraps her arms around her legs and tucks her face behind her knees. I swivel round next to her, in a similar position, with my back to the front door. We've been staring down the dark corridor for a long time when she finally speaks:

"Remember when we took him to the duck pond and he shouted, '*A golden fish!*' and that whole family smiled at us? Even the kids."

"And then he kept saying it because he knew it was cute."

"Yes. Was that the day when he first saw a caterpillar? What was that sound he used to make?"

"*Woooaaah*," I say, impersonating Charlie.

Lyd starts to laugh but chokes up with sadness.

We reflect a while.

It's the first time she's started a conversation with a memory of Charlie in over a year. For months after I got back from the psychiatric ward almost every silence was followed by, 'Remember when...' He could come up in the middle of anything: talking about the electricity bill, making a cup of tea, watching the shadow of the television pass along the carpet. Our grief was so all encompassing that remembering him was the only thing we were ever really doing.

After about six months Lyd didn't want to talk about Charlie anymore. She turned her back on the idea of him, wouldn't visit his grave, closed his bedroom door, and punished me with terrible moods if I brought him up. Even these days she doesn't really like to talk about him so this mentioning of him seems like a step forward.

"I know it sounds stupid," she says, eventually breaking the silence, "but I didn't believe I could get pregnant again. I thought that part of me was dead. I never even imagined... In my head, we were these shadow people, and all we could ever have was a shadow life. That's one of the reasons why we had to stay together. It wouldn't be fair to whoever we met next. It wouldn't be real. You know?"

27

"Sure."

I put my arm over her shoulders.

"But now, with this… I don't want to be some kind of shadow family. It's not right. It's not how it's supposed to be."

"It doesn't have to be like that."

"How could it be any other way?" she asks.

"It's impossible to know how a baby will change things."

"Maybe."

"This could be the best thing for us."

"I doubt that," she says.

"But maybe it's time for us to start trying a little harder?"

She nods and looks at me with a frown.

"Why are your hands shaking?"

I look at my right hand on her shoulder. The tremble has expanded into a shake.

"I haven't really eaten properly today," I say, pulling the hand away from her. I try for humour, "And it's emotional, down here, behind the front door."

She smiles, with love, sadness, but also an unanswered question behind it all.

"Come on," I say, shifting the weight off my pelvis. "Let's get up."

She begins to stand. I rise with her.

"What's for dinner?" she asks. "Do you want me to make something?"

"I've not really thought about it. There's that leftover curry."

"Sounds good."

We walk in the dark towards the kitchen. My hand hovers along the wall and starts feeling for the plastic of the light switch. I stop, stroke up and down, move my hand around in circles. It seems to have moved. Lyd steps up and reaches for where she thinks it is but she doesn't find it either. We grope around in the shadows for a few seconds.

"Is this even the right wall?" she asks.

"I can't remember," I say. "Is it over there?"

TWO

Not many animals adapted to the cities but certain kinds of scavengers thrive on human waste: pigeons, rats, mice and squirrels. Foxes too, with their guile and their burrows, made headway. But something happened to these animals in the transition. They became dirty and dishevelled, sooty and infested. However, one of the earliest colonisers managed to maintain its natural dignity: the common blackbird. After hundreds of years living in cities the civilisation still slips right off them. Sometimes a person hears one singing the song of the car alarm or the mobile phone but these whistles are not the tainted echoes of the technological era, they are full of imitative joy. The blackbirds are singing about a subject larger than the city, the thing above and below it, inside and out: boundless, endless Nature.

Two weeks later. Saturday morning. There's no ice on the ground but it's still cold. Lyd is out shopping for a meal for her family. We're going to break the news to them tonight. Most people wait a couple of months but Lyd is too close to them to keep anything big like this quiet.

I stand in the back garden drinking my morning coffee with a pack of sultanas in the pocket of my dressing gown. A week ago I bought a separate supply especially for the blackbirds so that Lyd wouldn't notice our normal pack depleting. I keep them hidden at the back of the tea towel drawer. I don't know why.

"Blackie," I say, following with a quick, fluctuating whistle.

He flies out of our evergreen and down onto the lawn. I throw out a single sultana at a time and smile continuously as he chases after them. He's become very used to my presence. The sliding of the screen door doesn't scare him away and he happily lets me stand and watch him. The others only play or eat on the grass if I sit down and remain very still.

Lyd has told me in advance that she'll be stressing out and that it will probably be better if we stay out of each other's way until people start arriving at 7pm so, when I hear her car in the driveway, I quickly come in from the garden, stash my sultanas at the back of the tea towel drawer, run upstairs and go to my office.

The novelty and excitement of my new ideas have passed but my need to keep writing the story is still great. I imagine it similar to how an archaeologist must feel when his tool first strikes an ancient set of bones. Exhilaration comes first, having found something rare, but that is short lived. The real work still needs to be done.

The trick is to let the hidden object do the talking: sense its lines, move unflinchingly along its curves, allow something deeper to take over, work selflessly and relentlessly until you gradually reveal something alien and unimagined. That's the stage I'm entering: climbing down into my writer's pit and scraping and brushing the bones of my story every day.

I write and edit in my office all day whilst she prepares for her family's arrival. I make sure I'm done by 5:30pm to give myself plenty of time to lift my head out of the writing pit and get cleaned up. I wear my smartest jeans, a checked cotton shirt and brown suede ankle boots.

Lyd's parents, Fee and Dom, arrive first with their overnight bags and a display of civility and goodwill that cleverly disguises their concerns about the fact that their whole family has been invited over on the same night. They are both dressed in simple and inscrutable smart-casual clothing chosen logically and with candour for exactly this sort of occasion.

We sit them down in the living room and serve Prosecco in champagne flutes, which they receive delightedly. After spending a couple of minutes welcoming them and asking about their journey, Lyd excuses herself and goes back to the kitchen. I ask them what they're currently reading and we arrive at the next ringing of the doorbell without any awkward pauses.

It's Jayne at the door, Lyd's big sister, Fee and Dom's middle child. She's brought a bottle of red wine and a worried curiosity that she's masking in amusement.

I take her coat.

She's wearing an electric-blue pencil skirt, an eighties' blouse with an eye-straining black-and-white pattern, yellow tights and shiny red brogues. "Clashing" is her style, and it oddly opposes her facilitating nature.

In a social context, Jayne almost always focuses on putting the most nervous and uncomfortable person in a group at ease. When we first met, I thought she really liked me. Now I'm a little bit ashamed of how long it took her to move on from looking after me.

After getting Jayne a glass of Prosecco, I help Lyd in the kitchen whilst those three catch up in the front room. Her stress levels are peaking and her creased brow-line means she's feeling emotionally vulnerable so I stay quiet, only asking for new jobs when she's pausing for breath.

She asks me to watch the hobs whilst she pops upstairs to change and reappears less than five minutes later in a sleeveless red dress with a high neck, dark tights and a pair of black ballerina flats. She looks great and I tell her this but she's already worrying about the food again.

The doorbell rings.

It's Lyd's brother, Peter, the eldest. He's brought a date who hasn't been invited. This is typical of Peter. Lyd envisioned an intimate meal where she could carefully tell her immediate family that she's expecting a baby. Now it's going to be an evening about meeting Peter's new girlfriend.

"Come in. They're all through here."

Peter's inflated sense of self-worth makes me despair and I find it impossible to understand how nobody else can see that he clearly has a drug problem; cocaine and benzodiazepines, I think. I also hate the way he parades women around in front of his family as though his vulgar prowess says nothing about his emotional problems or his inability to commit to a relationship.

The worst thing is that they all devour his charm hook, line and sinker. Even Lyd, a perfect critic of all things patriarchal, has a blind spot where he's concerned. I once made a blasé crack about the fact that he always wears Prada suits because he's a narcissistic egomaniac and Lyd got depressed for a week because she didn't know how to forgive me.

"Vincey Vince Vincent and the Vince Watergate Band," he says, with his arms open – this is his jovial way of greeting me and simultaneously saying that I'm a pathetic creative egotist.

(Watergate is my surname which, unlike most terrible surnames, escaped ridicule and attention until it captured the imaginations of the freaks and geeks at university.)

"Hello, Peter," I reply, not taking the bait and certainly not moving into his giant arm span to be crushed by an overzealous and impersonal hug.

"This is Pascale."

"Nice to meet you."

I extend a hand

"And you," she says, taking the hand for a second, very sweetly.

She's a nervous creature but the pinch of the thumb says sensual and self-possessed too. She is petite, has a slight French accent, a dark bob haircut and is wearing a simple black dress. As usual, Peter has ensnared a beautiful and intelligent young woman.

I close the front door (Peter uses these two seconds to grope Pascale, as though my eyes lack peripheral vision) and then they follow me through the hall to the living room.

"Guess who?" I say into the living room doorway.

They cheer for Peter's visage when it appears before them.

"Rumours of my death have been greatly exaggerated," says Peter, motioning with his hands for his admiring fans to now sit down.

They all laugh, relishing his irony.

Pascale creeps out from behind him with a coy smile, clutching a bottle of gin.

"And here is my exquisite aperitif," he says. "The young French lady holding it is called Pascale."

Even though he has introduced her like a misogynistic gameshow host, there is another bout of laughter.

"Pay no attention to him," says Jayne, rising to introduce herself to Pascale whilst Fee and Dom look her up and down with vacant smiles.

"I'll go set another space," I say. "Drinks, anyone?"

"A G&T would go down a treat," says Peter, snagging the gin from Pascale and passing it to me.

"Oh, yes," agrees Fee.

"Mmm," confirms Dom.

Jayne and Pascale, great friends in seconds, spare a moment to nod.

"Five Gee and Tees," I say, walking to the kitchen to prepare them.

"Peter?" asks Lyd.

"And *Pascale*."

"You're kidding?"

"Afraid not."

"What am I going to do?"

"I'm just making them all a gin and tonic then I'll set another place at the table. You want one?"

"Yes. But I can't, can I?"

"Sorry, honey. I forgot."

33

"Shit. Shit. Shit."

"It's going to be fine."

Lyd's face freezes in a distorted grimace. It can go one of two ways from here: angry meltdown or resilience. She rubs her forehead with the back of a hand that holds a large kitchen knife.

"There's not going to be enough food," she says.

Resilience.

"We'll make it stretch," I reply.

"Squiddy-pants," says Peter, entering the kitchen.

"Isn't it bad luck to see the chef before the dinner?" I ask, cutting lemons for the drinks, buying Lyd a couple of valuable seconds.

"Nonsense."

He approaches her.

She relaxes, becomes his loving little sister and embraces him, still holding the knife.

"Hey, bro."

"I hope you don't mind, I brought a guest."

"I don't, but a little bit of warning wouldn't have gone amiss. I'm cooking for six here."

"I *literally* couldn't. She just got back from France two hours ago. I didn't think she'd make it. Besides, she eats like a mouse. I promise."

"She better. Now, shoo. I'm busy."

Peter does as he's told with a cheeky grin and a wink.

I serve the gin and tonics and take out a small tray of smoked salmon with cream cheese on tiny pieces of rye bread. They are all happy and chatting so I put a collection of Bach's cello suites on quietly in the background for them.

Back in the kitchen I set a seventh place at our four-seater kitchen table.

"Do you still want to tell them?" I ask.

"I think so," says Lyd. "Let's see how it goes. Maybe a stranger will make it more normal."

"That's true." I walk over and kiss her. "I hadn't thought of that."

"We're almost ready here."

"I'll just pop up and get my office chair for Pascale, then I'll call them through."

"Go on then, quick."

I run up and grab the chair and, as I rush out onto the landing, I almost knock into Charlie playing in the hall. I turn my hips to the side, raise the chair a little and say:

"Oopsy-daisy."

When I get to the top of the stairs I stop dead and all the hairs on my arms and neck rise. I don't dare look back. I take a deep breath, walk downstairs and stand in the living room doorway.

My head is still upstairs on the landing. I didn't actually see Charlie, I reason. His face was not part of the experience. It was just the notion of his presence, an awareness of his body filling space. Not a hallucination, something else.

When I become aware of myself again everybody is looking at me vacantly holding an office chair in the doorway.

"Dinnertime," I say.

Dom gives Fee a look of concern, seemingly referring to something they've spoken about earlier. Jayne glances at me and then focuses on taking Pascale's attention away from me. Peter stares at me like a car crash, brimming with morbid pleasure. Realising I'm now redundant, I turn from them, distracted, and head to the kitchen to put the chair in place.

The silence I created behind me soon fills up with chatter again. I sit down. Lyd says something but I don't hear it.

Did I actually see anything? The top of his head?

"*Vince.*"

"Hmm?"

"Can you grab these soups?"

I nod and stand up as the group comes through.

"You guys take the chairs. Me and Vince will sit on the stools," calls Lyd.

They arrange themselves around the table and I begin playing waiter.

"What's this?" asks Fee.

"Oh, erm. Soup," I say.

Peter laughs out loud.

"French onion," calls Lyd, looking at me with confused derision.

It was just a silly moment, I tell myself. People imagine things all the time. They just don't speak about them.

The table is cramped with seven of us. Pascale apologises for her presence. Fee says she is being silly and Dom says it's cosy, rubbing her shoulder in a way that makes Pascale uncomfortable and Jayne explode with laughter.

The conversation starts with the usual pleasantries about the food but soon takes a detour into the current state of left-wing politics. I slowly become engaged again (I catch Lyd looking at me approvingly). Everyone is pleased that Pascale has a humanitarian agenda and briefly feels sorry for her when Peter takes pains to expose the naïvety of her position on global poverty.

After this, Lyd serves goat's cheese and roasted pine nuts on rocket and we all isolate Peter from the conversation for a while. Jayne and Pascale continue to hit it off, laughing whilst me and Lyd speak to her parents about whether or not they are making the most of their retirement.

Once everybody has finished the starter Lyd puts her hand on my leg. She's getting nervous (I presume she intends to make a toast before the main meal). I rub the top of her hand and give her a sympathetic smile. She refills her glass of wine; something tells me it's not the first time but I make no attempt to confront her about it even though I know I should.

I help clear the plates and set up the table for the main dish. I manage to get Lyd to myself in a spot by the cooker.

"How are you feeling?" I ask, putting my hand on her hip.

"It is what it is," she says.

"Are you going to say something before we eat?"

She nods.

I kiss her quickly and take two trays of chunky cod fillets that have been cooking in white wine, garlic, cream and capers over to the table. Everybody makes appreciative sounds as they see the size and amount of cod and smell the aroma drifting around them.

I put the potatoes and green vegetables in the centre of the table whilst Lyd serves out the fish. Then I top up everybody's wine, put another bottle of white and red on the table and sit down. Lyd remains standing and puts her hand on my shoulder. Peter shoves a large mouthful of cod into his mouth.

"Before we begin," says Lyd, raising her glass. "We have an announcement to make…" She chokes up, almost crying, and looks down at me. "Vince? Could you?"

I stand up and put my arm around her.

"It's been a tough couple of years, as you all know, and it wasn't planned, but now it's happened we're going ahead. It feels like the right thing to do… Lyd's pregnant."

"How beautiful," says Pascale, clasping her hands together adorably before noticing the quiet anxiety in the room all around her.

The toast disintegrates. Nobody raises their glass.

"Good for you, honey," says Dom, suddenly kicking into gear and having a semi-symbolic sip of his drink. "It's time to move on."

As Lyd raises an unimpressed bottom lip to her father's response, Jayne, cringing humorously at him, stands up and walks round to give her a hug.

"I love you so much, Squid," she says to Lyd. "Let me know a good day for lunch next week."

Lyd nods and they kiss each other on both cheeks. Jayne continues her response by moving towards me.

"Check you out, Mr Fertile!" She prods my side, smiles widely, and expands her arms for a quick hug that connects at the collar bone (at which point she whispers), "I hope it all seems manageable, darling."

"Thanks," I say, touched but mildly offended.

Fee is still in quiet contemplation. Pascale is looking at Peter with a question mark on her forehead and Peter is shaking his head subtly to say, *Not now*. Dom is wringing his hands with a nervous smile waiting for his wife to say something.

"Of course, it's great news," says Fee, finally realising that things are now resting on her response. "Congratulations."

She doesn't get up. She descends straight back into deep thought. Lyd's face droops into disappointment and then fights back, deciding to find it all amusing. She looks at me and raises her eyebrows. I mirror her expression, kiss her and we both sit down.

"Congrats, sis," says Peter, in an untouched tone.

"Thanks, bro," says Lyd, impersonating him in a robotic monotone (to which he raises his glass and swallows half of his wine in one gulp).

Maybe I'm being paranoid but the message I'm receiving is, *Poor Lydia. She's well and truly stuck with him now.*

There's much more introspection throughout the rest of the meal. Pascale's eyes are flitting around from face to face nervously. Peter is scowling with amusement, as though life is a series of sadistic jokes and the punchline, today, is that his little sister has been impregnated by me... again. Dom and Fee are busy mentally reforming the essence of their united front. Jayne continually fails to engage anyone with whatever comes to her mind. I start thinking about Charlie playing upstairs on the landing. Lyd is becoming so visibly upset that, one by one, all any of us are thinking is, *Please don't cry.*

Eventually, the cello suites in the other room finish and, even though we've barely been able to hear them, the silence they leave behind is cavernous. Somebody has to speak and this is exactly the kind of time when I'm no good at talking. We wait, most of us taking a moment to glance at Lyd. I can hear myself chewing and so begin moving my jaw more delicately. The sound of cutlery on plates is excruciating.

"Remember, whenever it got tense, Charlie would just burst out laughing like a maniac?" says Lyd, laughing sadly.

Jayne almost chokes on her food with relief and joy. Everybody else looks more anxious.

"I remember that," says Jayne. "He was a right little psycho."

Fee and Dom both look at me cautiously, obviously equating Charlie's maniacal streak with me. I ignore them and smile at Lyd.

"He got that from his aunty," I say.

"Hey!" protests Jayne.

"No," I grant her. "Not really. He always laughed like a villain, didn't he? No matter what he was laughing at."

"Charlie was their son," Peter whispers to Pascale.

Pascale frowns with sadness and pity.

"He was so weird," says Lyd. "Half the time we had no idea what he was laughing about."

Again, Fee and Dom glance my way. It annoys me the second time because they both loved Charlie deeply. Underneath their silent insinuation that he was a bizarre boy because of me there rests the faintest allegation about the unpredictability of his cancer and death.

"What do you miss about him?" I ask in their direction.

"Oh, the whole lot," says Fee. "That cheeky look in his eyes. He could get round anybody with that look."

Me and Lyd smile. We know the look she means.

"Oh yes," agrees Peter. "Butter wouldn't melt anywhere near him. He could turn shit to gold, that one."

We all laugh.

"He was an extremely crafty young boy," says Dom. "A trickster. Not many children can make me laugh but he always managed it."

This is the first time we've reminisced about Charlie as a family. Since the conversation has been broached there's no going back. We carry on drinking and start telling stories about him, forgetting about dessert until it gets late. We apologise to Pascale half a dozen times but then carry on. We speak for so long and with such good cheer that everything seems alright again.

When Peter decides to call it a night, and Jayne follows suit, it's agreed by everyone that a lovely night has been had. We set up a double mattress in the living room for Dom and Fee and say goodnight with smiles on our faces.

It's only afterward, lying in bed, that the evening begins to seem gloomy. The new baby barely made an impact. Nobody even mentioned the pregnancy at the end of the night.

Lyd is out like a light, exhausted from all the cooking and worrying, but I find it impossible to sleep. Since I've cut out my lithium I'm struggling to get six hours a night. This evening it's worse still. I have indigestion, cold sweats and I'm inadvertently drunk. Black waves of dizziness crash against my skull, the world spins out of control, icy oceans rise into the sky.

I roll around for hours until my legs are aching.

When the tides of drunken chaos finally settle the blackbirds are singing outside. I hear Blackie up on our drainpipe, and maybe six or seven other blackbirds that are further away. The dark tales of winter are gone from his song. It's more matter of fact now.

It's all going to be starting soon, his tone says.

My ears release their focus and I listen to the entire dawn chorus for a while. Is it a giant conversation, parts of it whistled across from Asia? A grouping of territorial sound barriers? A musical collaboration? Calls of romantic longing? Utter randomness? Ancient black secrets?

Lyd wakes me up with a nudge.

"Come on, Vince. Time to get up. They're both up and showered."

My eyes feel like they have knitting needles in them. I can't have slept for more than a couple of hours.

"How much did you drink last night?" she asks, seeing the struggle on my face.

"Couldn't sleep."

She sighs.

"Okay. They've already had cereal and want to get out. I'll take them for a walk on the Heath. They want to buy us lunch before they go. You've got two hours."

"They'll be glad to get you on your own."

"Two hours."

"Thank you."

I sense her eyes rolling but sleep still has its hooks in me. I slip out of the bedroom and back into the blackness.

"*Vince*? Are you not even up? You've had nearly three hours."

"Huh?"

"It's almost twelve. Come on. You're not exactly doing much to save your image here."

"I'm up," I say, swinging my legs over the edge of the bed and sitting up with my eyes still closed. "Sorry."

I stumble to the bathroom and have a quick shower, mulling over Lyd's "save your image" comment.

When I get downstairs, Fee and Dom smile but their eyes are wondering how I look as bad as I do given that we all went to bed at the same time. Seeing how alert and vitalised they are makes me want to crawl into a cave and disappear for a month.

"Morning," I say.

"Only just," says Lyd.

"You didn't sleep well?" asks Dom.

"I'll live."

"Glad to hear it," says Fee.

We walk up Archway Road for lunch at a local café that does expensive Italian breads, niche fillings, strong coffees and fresh juices. Fee and Dom both ask for the daily special: baked eggs on spinach with Parmesan and tomato toast. Fee wants an apple, pear and cherry juice and Dom a blueberry, strawberry and apple juice. Lyd orders tomato, mozzarella and pesto in piadina with an orange, mango and banana smoothie. I get a Parma ham ciabatta and a double espresso.

The conversation is stilted. Fee and Dom drink their juice in sharp, bitter sips. It's obvious they've been talking about me all morning.

I'm sighing a lot. Lyd keeps looking at me. I can't think of anything to say. One thing is clear; nobody wants to talk about the baby.

As my sandwich arrives I anxiously reach up to take the plate from the waiter and see that my hand is trembling quite badly. I recall my arm as casually as possible (not very) and he puts the plate down with a quizzical smile.

Thankfully, everybody else's food is served within moments, distracting them from my weird arm flinch, but Dom manages to flick a surly glance my way before smiling and nodding gratefully for his baked eggs.

"So my writing's going really well at the moment," I say.

Dom coughs and splutters. He's choking on his first bite of Parmesan and tomato toast. To be fair, it does look very dry but it feels like he's choking on my ambitions.

The cough turns into a fit, which slowly settles and then has a second wave. Fee pats his back and glares at me with scathing disinterest. She does this for so long that I look over my shoulder and see that there is absolutely nothing offensively boring behind me. Finally, Dom catches his breath.

"But you're not really ready to talk about it yet, are you, honey?" says Lyd.

"No, I guess not."

The coffee is not working. Tiredness is draining all the accuracy from my perceptions. Everything is grey and dull. My eyes are lilting.

"Lydia tells us that you had an interview last month. Writing campaign copy for Freedom From Torture, was it?"

Fee inhales violently up through her nose. This throws me off. Did she ask or did he? I answer into my sandwich.

"Hmm, yes. It was quite a tortuous interview, actually."

Nobody laughs.

"I didn't get it."

"He does apply for things when he sees something he likes," says Lyd.

I flash a quick frown at her.

"There's just so little in the world I seem to like."

I say this looking directly at Fee. Her throat does a small, repulsed lift. Dom watches her in anticipation. Lyd squeezes my thigh. I'm about to take a bite of my sandwich but a deep tremor in my right hand and arm means I barely get the thing anywhere near my mouth. I pretend I'm looking at the bread, admiring it close up, and then put it down on my plate with a bit too much of a clatter.

"A household needs two fixed incomes these days though, doesn't it?" says Fee. "Not everybody has the luxury of choosing a job they like."

"But some jobs barely cover the cost of childcare, do they?" I reply.

"Some of your three-month royalty cheques barely seem to cover one week's shopping," says Fee.

"It's tough for your generation. We're not denying that," says Dom, pulling my angry glare off his wife.

"And we appreciate everything you've done for us," I say, through gritted teeth.

We eat in silence.

My ciabatta is tough and floury. The taste of Parma ham is hardly noticeable. I've finished my coffee and my mouth is getting dry. They all have big glasses full of fresh juice, colours so bright they're searing my eyes. I cough a floury cough.

"Maybe something else will come up," I say.

This is my first mild appeasement and Lyd rewards me for it with a quick touch of the shoulder.

"Let's hope so," says Fee.

Her tiny snipe makes me want to slam my arm down on the table, swipe all the stuff off it and rage-tip every object in the restaurant over. I'm clenching my teeth and trying to smile. I recall that this isn't the first time I've felt like this in the last few weeks and tell myself to calm down because I'm suddenly warning myself, *Irrational violence is a symptom of mania*.

I try to bring it down a notch. I breathe slowly, chew through my tough floury bread, and ease into a calmer self. I say and do nothing and gradually revert to the prior tired mess.

After this wave of anger the meal doesn't get any better, worse or any more interesting. Lyd manages to grab the conversation and take its focus off me.

"Wasn't Pascale lovely?"

"Her English was perfect."

"Oh, yes, great girl."

Luckily, my weird hands seem to be flying beneath the radar but there's a definite sense of my oddness getting through. I'm still getting glances from Fee. It's taking a great effort for me to remain within the parameters of normal social decorum. I can barely chew and swallow properly, let alone sit up straight.

"And so pretty too."

"I just hope we get to meet this one again."

Why is nobody talking about the baby? I want to scream all of a sudden, my rage popping back out for an encore. I clench my teeth and breathe slowly through my nose, closing my eyes. They carry on singing Pascale's praises.

It's obvious why the baby is not up for discussion. There's something very concise getting in the way of making it an appropriate subject: me. I am the priority problem. The baby is the next problem.

They think it's selfish and irresponsible for me to want anything besides an income and some stability but my mind is fast and clear for the first time in years. I have to keep writing my new novel. I have to prove that I don't need lithium. I can't be a father who gave up on himself.

THREE

When the air loses its chill and the courtship rituals of the mating season begin, life of almost every kind begins to thrive. Tiny curled up leaves bud on tree branches. Tulips, daffodils and bluebells rise bravely. Early birds scurry in the undergrowth looking for the next special twig that looks like home. On any given day a million flying insects might suddenly burst into the skies as though a secret voice, connected to the dreams of every one of their kind, has called, 'Wake up! Your wings are ready! It's time to fly! It's time to fly!'

I'm listening to Bessie Smith whilst I eat my breakfast in the kitchen. The sliding door is open, letting in cool, fresh air. An ineffective sun is shining in a mostly blue sky. Blackie's on the lawn courting a slender brown female with a slightly speckled breast. He's dancing around her, running with his head bowed and beak open, singing a strange low song. This morning ritual has been going on for days.

After putting my empty bowl in the sink and grabbing my sultanas, I stand on the lawn in my dressing gown and slippers. The two birds fly into the evergreen when I step onto the patio but when I give my usual whistle, Blackie pops out, lands on the lawn and chirps at me.

– *chink-chink, chook-chook, chink-chink, chook-chook* –

(I've taken to loosely interpreting him and imagine this frequent and distinctive chirp he sends my way means both *Hello* and *Goodbye*.)

I warm him up by throwing single sultanas for him to chase after (he occasionally lets out a little chirp of protest if he feels the distance was too far between the two).

After a few minutes the real training begins. I leave a sultana on the edge of the patio and stand back. He jumps up and gobbles it down. I move forward and put another one down but closer to the house. He flutters back to the middle of the lawn.

– *pook-pook-pook, che-che-chook* –

(*You're too close*.)

I move back a little.

He jumps onto the patio, eyes up the situation, slowly edges forward and then runs and grabs the next sultana. Once he has it he rushes back to the edge of the patio.

I leave one even closer to my feet this time. He flies onto the lawn again.

– *pook-pook-pook, che-che-chook, pook-pook-pook* –

(*Way too close*.)

I move back a tiny bit. The sultana is about half a metre away from me. He climbs onto the patio, goes left, looks at it, goes right, looks at it. He takes a hop. He's really close. He lunges in for the sultana, runs away quickly, but stays on the patio looking at me, wondering what kind of game I'm playing.

I take a step back, into the house, and leave a sultana outside on the patio, another on the small white ledge beside the sliding door and one inside on the kitchen lino. He slowly hops diagonally left, diagonally right, diagonally left again. He twists his head to analyse the situation and decides he can risk the first one. He jumps over to it.

I can't see him because he's too close to the house. I wait, stretching onto my tiptoes, watching the ledge. I wonder if he's hopped away. I'm about to go and check when he jumps up onto it. I smile. He looks sideways at me, down at the sultana, back at me and then eats it. He sees the sultana on the lino but hops back onto the patio.

– pook-pook, chickachicka-choo-choo, choo-chook –
(*I don't trust you enough yet.*)

I repeat this previous step but the first sultana I leave out is the one on the ledge. I put three more on the lino inside the kitchen. He eats the first sultana but stops on the threshold, stares inside for a while and goes back onto the patio. I put another sultana on the ledge and stand back. The same thing happens.

The third time, after eating the first sultana and staring at the others for twenty or thirty seconds, he finally hops into the house and takes a sultana off the lino. He then immediately flutters back out onto the lawn (because I accidentally release a loud breath of delight).

Over the course of an hour I repeat this exercise again and again but, up on the edge of the breakfast counter, I place a big pile of sultanas in his direct line of sight. When he gets comfortable coming inside I only leave one sultana between the sliding doors and the breakfast counter and sit down on the stool furthest from the big pile of sultanas. He comes in for the single sultana four times, staying inside and eyeing up the big pile for longer and longer until, on the fifth time, he finally flies up onto the counter and buries his beak in the heap.

I am frozen on my stool but ecstatic. My spine is tense. I daren't even move my head. His attempt to eat from the counter causes about ten or fifteen sultanas to fall to the floor. Even though he has made this commotion, the sound of their dropping onto the lino unsettles him.

– pook-pook, twit-ta-twer-choo-choo, twit-ta-tewah-tewah –
(*I don't like this anymore. That's enough for today.*)

He jumps off the counter and flies out the door, across the garden and back into the evergreen. I can't stop smiling for about fifteen minutes. The spike in my happiness makes me decide that today is the day that I'm going to pack up Charlie's room. Our baby is only the size of a grain of rice but I've been off the lithium for a month and suddenly feel capable of facing it. I want to do it before the feeling goes. I'm more and more aware that it has to become the baby's room as soon as possible. It's time for things to change.

The local shop doesn't have any cardboard boxes. I have no luck at the supermarket either. I don't believe the woman who tells me (she's very distracted, asking every colleague who passes if they've seen Shaniqua, and she's unwilling to leave her post) but there's nothing I can do about it. She has a special way of standing guard against my need to progress into the store and ask somebody else, a silent threat. I have to concede to the fact that free things no longer exist and spend an unbearable amount of money in a shop that is tagged on to the front of a storage facility. The boxes are good quality and they all match so this offsets some of the resentment of paying.

Back home, I mentally prepare for the task at hand, warning myself that sentiment and nostalgia are the enemies of efficient packing. I try to enter Charlie's room with my emotions on mute. The first thing that has to go, before I start filling boxes, is the low-hanging moon. This dead pendulum has the ability to ruin the momentum of the entire day. It is too unique and holds too many special memories.

When Charlie's garbled toddler noises began turning into understandable words and phrases it quickly became apparent that he had been waiting to tell me that he wanted to play Fire Engines on the Moon. I never got to the bottom of why he was so inexplicably obsessed with the idea of this game but I was always quietly proud of how much imagination it displayed. He requested the game so often that I ended up making him a moon. I took two square cushions from the couch, lots of scrunched up newspaper, and wrapped it all in lots of string and sticky tape. Then I gave it a surface covering of white printer paper and hung it from a hook in the ceiling. It swung about a foot from the floor so it was easy for Charlie to play with but just slightly too high for him to climb on. Being so low, it also gave him the opportunity to imagine that it was part of the sky that emanated from his planetary carpet.

Slowly but surely I decorated it, at Charlie's request, with craters, roads for the fire engines and some of his other random inspirations (a lollipop lady, a shipwreck, Big Ben). He loved his moon.

When he didn't want to play Fire Engines on the Moon it also served as an excellent wrecking ball. Decimating piles of his books and toys gave him lots of pleasure and I would frequently hear him laughing on his own at the naughtiness of it all.

Whenever I carefully chastised him about this destructive game he would protest his innocence by saying, Moon Around the World. This was his way of suggesting that an interesting and fun science experiment (that I initiated by showing him how orbits work) had gone a little bit wrong. He always managed to distance himself from trouble in this way, not because he believed in the validity of deceit but because he knew that I would find his lies amusing.

I unhook the moon and hold it in my hands, staring at it for a while. I think about keeping it, packing it in a box, but remember my initial ruling – no sentiment and no nostalgia. I bring a pair of scissors up from downstairs and begin to cut into it.

It's been so long since I made it that the colour of the two cushions inside it is more vibrant than the ones downstairs. I pat them down, fluff them up and put them back in the living room. I put the rest of the scraps in a bin bag.

It was a good decision. After this I feel capable of dealing with anything the room can possibly throw at me. The entrance to the attic is in Charlie's room so I clear as I go, climbing up and down the ladder all afternoon; a box of clothes, a box of bedding, two boxes of toys, one box of books with all his pictures and paintings on top, a box of cuddly toys (horrible ferret teddy included), two trips for the dismantled toy chest, one for the toy whiteboard.

It's going really well. I've got every loose object packed up. The boxes are labelled with marker pens, stacked neatly. Everything is in its place. I just have the bulky furniture to deal with. Then I notice the windowsill. The retro 1960s robot should be in a toy box but the toy boxes are taped up and at the bottom of a pile of boxes in the attic. This single, defiant object brings the gravity of the situation falling upon me.

In violent despair, I grab the wardrobe and heave it over. It crashes into the middle of the room. I grab the retro 1960s robot and jump onto the back of it, smashing the robot down again and again. Somewhere along the way the MDF backing cracks and I fall into the main body. Trying to destroy the rest is difficult. I keep stubbing my fingertips and knuckles. When my thumb cracks on a side panel I cry out in pain and stop. The robot doesn't have a scratch on it. I drop it in with the rubble.

My arms are full of adrenalin. I fall over trying to stand up. Looking at the mess I've made, I begin concocting the most plausible lie for Lyd: I had to smash it because it wouldn't fit in the attic. All the dints on the main body, I'm not so sure about. I'll probably have to work things so that it never sees the light of day again.

By the time I hear the front door open downstairs I've taken up the sides and doors of the wardrobe, filled a bin bag with broken pieces of MDF and tossed the retro 1960s robot behind the piles of boxes in the attic. I'm in the process of taking screws out of the slats on the child-sized bed.

I try to stay calm about Lyd being home but immediately fail. Blood rushes to my head as I hear her on the stairs. My arms feel light and jittery. My hands begin trembling. I try to maintain my conviction about my decision to do all this but I suddenly want to cry.

She is craning her neck to see if I'm in my writing room as she passes but then stops dead, noticing that Charlie's bedroom door is open.

"No," she says, looking through the doorway.

She's wearing her black trouser suit with a white blouse which either means she woke in a highly emotional state and needed the suit to feel solid and professional or she had an important and stressful meeting today. Whichever it was, there is gloom in her eyes and it's rapidly expanding into damnation.

"I can't believe you did this."

She walks away.

"It had to be done," I call after her, getting up and moving into the corridor.

She stops before our bedroom door and turns back to face me: vacant, inhuman. I stay by Charlie's doorway, defending my decision to box up the room.

"I know you're not ready for this," I say, "but we have to face what's coming."

She walks up to me.

"I don't have to face anything," she says.

She punctuates the sentence by pushing me in the chest. I stumble back and jar my spine on the doorframe. After looking at the floor for a couple of seconds, trying to calm herself, Lyd launches at me, flapping her arms wildly.

"Heartless. Bastard."

"Stop. Stop!"

I grab her wrists and restrain her.

"There was still time," she whimpers, limp and instantly defeated now that I've grabbed her.

"Time for what?"

"It's not too late."

I move my head, trying to gain eye contact. She evades my attempts.

"I don't have to go through with it," she says.

"Go through with what?"

"I don't have to keep the baby."

"An abortion?"

"It's my body," she says, looking off to the side.

"But… we told your family."

She turns away from me but doesn't walk off.

"Is that what you really want?" I ask, putting my hand on her upper arm.

Her shoulder flinches. I take my hand away.

"It's too late," she says. "We can't keep him now."

She walks into our bedroom. I follow.

"What are you talking about?"

"Forget it."

"It needed to be done. Baby or no baby. Do you really want an abortion?"

She sits on the bed and puts her face in her hands.

"I just want everything to stop, just for a minute. I'm tired, and nauseous. My whole body is sore. I have constant headaches. And you're on me as soon as I get through the door. The house is never empty. I've got this *thing* inside me. I'm never alone."

I'm trying to make my face express sympathy rather than confusion.

"I'm sorry," I say. "I'll give you more time to yourself."

"You should have told me…"

"I'm sorry."

"I didn't get a chance to say goodbye."

I sit by her on the bed.

"I'm sorry," I repeat. "I didn't think. Do you want to look through some of the boxes?"

"I don't want anything to do with it."

It's clear that she needs to be alone. I put my hand on her back for a moment. She looks repulsed by the physical contact so I stand up and leave the room. I think about going downstairs and making her a nice dinner but I have to stand by my decision so I go into Charlie's room and carry on dismantling his bed.

When I've put the pieces of the bed up in the attic and am in the process of sliding the ladder up into its mechanism, Lyd comes to the doorway. Seeing the room empty makes her turn her head away, raising one hand to her mouth and resting the other on her stomach.

"You should come in," I say.

"I can't even look at it."

I know what she means. My guts feel hollow. I step into the corridor and close the door behind me.

"I don't want an abortion," she says.

"No?"

"I don't know why I said that."

"No?"

"I know it's not… I need a drink. Do you want one?"

"Sure," I say, struggling not to reproach her for all the alcohol she's still drinking.

We go downstairs to the kitchen and she pours from an open bottle of Rioja. I wonder to myself when she opened it.

We sit at the kitchen table. After a large first sip, Lyd sighs with relief.

"I didn't mean to go crazy up there," she says. "I guess I thought we'd be using your study as the baby's room."

"I'm sorry. I thought it was the right thing to do. What about this abortion? This idea must have come from somewhere?"

"I'm tired. I was being spiteful. I hate feeling this irrational."

"Do you want to talk about it?"

She thinks for moment.

"The past keeps changing," she says.

"What do you mean?"

"Everything's slipping away. None of it's real. Last time, we were so young, so wrapped up in ourselves. We had no idea what it meant to be a family. We changed so fast, learnt things so quickly."

"We had to."

"There were all these new, spaces, inside me… When he was taken away they didn't disappear. I'm so lost inside myself. I'm a mother. You know? I never stopped being his mother."

"He wasn't taken," I say, correcting her.

"No," she confirms.

"Sorry, but I can't think of it like that."

"No. I know."

We pause.

"You'll always be his mother."

"But I'm not. I'm not a mother. Not anymore. Knowing that a part of our life with him was still here, that it was real, that was important to me."

"His room…"

"It's never going to feel like a baby's room. It's Charlie's room."

"We have to start looking forward. We have to try to make it feel right."

"Something in me was kept alive, knowing that all his things were behind that door; it was like Schrödinger's cat."

At this last remark she almost laughs but sighs grief through her nostrils instead.

"We can't cling to our old life. We have to get ready for our new one."

"I don't want it…"

I sip my wine quietly.

"The thing in Charlie's room," she says. "It's gone for ever. That part of me. I can't be that mother again. The mother I'm going to be. That's somebody else."

"Whatever's coming, we have to accept it."

"Why?"

"Because it's coming whether we like it or not," I say, raising my voice a little.

This hint of aggression does nothing but subdue Lyd further.

"I can feel it changing," she mumbles, before slugging down the last of her wine. "He's not here anymore."

"He was already gone."

"No, he wasn't," she says. "Not completely."

She stands up and leaves the kitchen. I look at the sliding

door absently, wondering how much of him I took away from her. I can faintly hear Blackie whistling up on the drainpipe. It soothes me to think of him out there, alone in the world, singing in the face of it all. Listening to him, I'm slowly guided back to the idea that packing up the room was the right thing to do.

FOUR

Lithium was one of the three stable elements synthesised in the moments of primordial fusion after the Big Bang. It rarely occurs freely in nature but there are traces of it in almost everything. Nucleosynthesis calculations present a "cosmological lithium discrepancy" because, in the atmosphere of dwarf stars, lithium abundance is often three times lower than expected. The amounts of hydrogen and helium (the other two stable elements synthesised) tally perfectly with predictions but the irregular lithium levels throw all of stellar physics and Big Bang nucleosynthesis into question.

Lyd is making a rocket, walnut and avocado salad. I'm pacing around the kitchen, being a bit useless. We're listening to Robert Johnson on the stereo. Whenever Lyd moves I seem to be standing in her way. Things have been strained since I packed up Charlie's room. Lyd seems to think that I've crossed a sacred line, undermined all the fundamental things we hold dear, and she's now applying the theory that I lack empathy to almost everything I do.

"I just think you should have told her in person," she says.

"What's the difference? I probably would have waited another two months if I didn't feel bad about the fact that your family already knew."

"You're constantly punishing her for remarrying, without even thinking about it."

"It didn't even occur to me that there was a proper way of doing it."

"Maybe it did," she says, scooping out an avocado. "Maybe it didn't."

"I've admitted that I'm not particularly bothered about seeing my stepdad and stepsister."

"John and Chelsea," she corrects me.

"She only ever calls me when they're both out the house. She cuts me short if I call when they're in."

"She's just trying to keep everybody happy. You want her all to yourself, and they want her all to themselves."

"In her eyes, I'm part of a previous life."

"We all have our separate lives."

I turn the music off.

"Are you ready?" I ask.

"Not really."

"Come on, I've been waiting ages."

"Fine," she says, putting down the knife, "but you can make the dressing."

We're griping at each other but I'm not going to let this ruin all my hard work. I've been building up to this moment for weeks. Lyd has promised she'll stay in the kitchen doorway, quiet and still. She moves into position.

I leave a small pile of sultanas on our breakfast counter, open the sliding door, sit on the usual stool and whistle. Seconds later Blackie flies out from the evergreen, across the lawn, through the open doorway and lands on the edge of our breakfast counter.

We've been eating our breakfast together like this most mornings. One day this week, when I slept in, I found him waiting at the sliding door and when I finally appeared he pecked at the glass to attract my attention.

He sees me sitting on my stool with a bowl in front of me, the usual pile of sultanas at his end, and presumes everything is normal. As promised, Lyd watches him peck at the sultanas silently from the kitchen doorway but only for about fifteen seconds before she says:

"This is really creepy."

Blackie looks at Lyd, back at me and releases a very angry and disapproving sound:

– *SEEEEE, POOK-POOK-POOK!* –

Then he flies back out of the sliding doors, across the lawn and into the evergreen.

"You annoyed him," I moan.

"And he annoyed me," she says. "I don't want his gross little bird feet on my breakfast counter. I don't know where he's been. What if he craps in here?"

"He doesn't. He won't. He's smarter than that."

"He's not smart. He's just figured out a new way of getting food."

"No," I say, "he likes coming in because he's brave. He's a risk-taker. He likes showing off."

"Why can't you make real friends instead of pretending some flea-ridden bird loves you?"

"I have real friends."

"I don't want you encouraging wild animals to come into my kitchen," she says. "It's weird."

"*Your* breakfast counter? *Your* kitchen?"

"You know what I mean."

"I think your parents are finally getting through to you."

"Don't be stupid. Of course they're not."

I realise that I want to talk about this even less than she does and so redirect our attention to the bird.

"I like having breakfast with him. It feels special, like it's a part of our new life."

She shakes her head and rolls her eyes.

"That sounds like it could be your mum outside."

"Lyd, don't be like this. I thought you'd think it was, I don't know, cool."

"Go and let your mum in."

I stand looking at her. The doorbell rings.

"Vince. Go."

"He's a good omen. I'm telling you."

I hear her mutter as I leave the room:

"Of course he is."

When I answer the door my mum's face erupts into a happiness that's going to be very difficult to follow through on. She rushes forward, puts her arms around my neck and makes a faux-excited vowel sound:

"*Eeeeeeeeeeeee.*"

"Hi, Mum."

She lets go and shuffles back with an excited wiggle to get a better look at me. She's wearing this season's Smart Look range from Next. Green and metallic tones, monochrome patches, premium fabric; she looks good but very much of the High Street. When I was little we were poor so now she treats herself.

John is looking up and down the street, unimpressed (as he is by everything). He wears grey old-man trousers (he's had them so long that I already know the rear seam is poorly restitched with white thread) and an untucked peach pastel shirt that the nineties forgot to take with them. If I had to signify the word boredom with one object it would be his large, drooping, grey moustache.

"John," I say, acknowledging him and holding out my hand.

"Vinny," he says, in his flat monotone, giving my hand one firm shake with a nod to match.

(Nobody calls me Vinny.)

"Little sis," I say to Chelsea.

She glances up from the screen of her mobile phone for half a second, screws up her face a little bit and then looks back down. She's wearing blue Nike tracksuit bottoms, Reebok classics and a cheap stripy sweater that says *C'est la vie* across the front in a handwritten font.

"Can I take madam's bag?" I ask her.

Chelsea takes a step away from me without looking up.

"Are you two okay?" my mum asks, looking into the house. "Where's Lydia?"

"Good, thanks," I say, taking her bag and grabbing John's from him. "She's in the kitchen."

"I hope she's not going to any trouble. We had Kentucky on the motorway. Didn't we, love?"

"Aye," says John. "We did."

"I'm sure it's fine," I say, ushering them in. "I'll just take your bags up."

Charlie's room is empty besides our visitor's double mattress and a chest of drawers. I stripped the wallpaper and whitewashed the walls at the start of the week. Every time I walk into the room I feel like my heart has been scraped out. Lyd hasn't even looked at it yet.

I drop the bags by the mattress and rush down to save Lyd from any social calamity that might be ensuing but, on the contrary, she's still in the kitchen and they have made themselves at home in the living room. The TV is already on and blaring out heinous advertisements. Lyd is putting cling film over the top of her bowl of salad. The kettle is on.

"Just making them a brew," she says, smiling at me with as little aggression as she can manage.

"Did they even say hello?"

"Your mum did."

"I can't believe they ate fried chicken on the way here," I say. "I told them you were making lunch."

"It's just a salad. It will keep for tomorrow... Or whenever."

"But you bought all that nice fresh bread."

"Forget about it. They're here now. Let's just try and keep them happy."

"Good luck."

Lyd smiles. She likes how anxious and critical I become around my family. It's a shame she's struggling to forgive me for Charlie's room.

"Remember, it's your mum you want to see. As long as she's alright."

I nod and kiss her on the cheek.

"Take these through."

I take the two teas to the living room and put them on the coffee table.

John already has his laptop out. Chelsea is still glued to her mobile phone. Mum is watching the TV. Their lifestyle is like a chain restaurant; everything around them is completely interchangeable. They have the charmless ability to pick up their world and somehow dump it in your front room within five seconds.

"Ta, love," says Mum, smiling gently and then raising both eyebrows and smiling with an extra ecstatic theatricality.

"Aye, ta," mumbles John, his face made even duller by the light emanating from his laptop.

"She drinks all this fancy coffee now," says Mum, rolling her eyes happily (which means Chelsea won't be happy unless she has a fancy coffee).

"Oh, right," I say. "What kind do you like?"

"You haven't got it," states Chelsea. "I like Starbucks."

"Lattes?"

"Aye, yeah, that's it. Latty."

"I'll see what I can do."

I go back to the kitchen.

"Chelsea wants a *latte*," I say with a smirk.

"Well, isn't she a very sophisticated fourteen-year-old girl?" says Lyd.

We eye each other wickedly. This visit could be good for us.

I make a filter coffee and warm some milk in the microwave.

"This is the best I can do, I'm afraid," I say, passing Chelsea my concoction.

Chelsea sneers over the rim of the cup, smells it and takes a sip. Pathetically, I'm eagerly awaiting her response.

"It's not like Starbucks," she says.

My mum lowers her head and smiles at Chelsea with a distinctly non-threatening face that nonetheless implies that she could perhaps, please, try to do a little bit better than that.

Chelsea sighs and takes another sip.

"It's good though," she says. "It's better than what she makes."

I put my hands together like a camp waiter, almost say, *Thank you*, restrain myself, and then walk back to Lyd in the kitchen.

"How long before they leave?" I ask.

She laughs.

An hour later we all get the Tube to Oxford Street. For Lyd's family eating together and being social is the main event but for my mum it's shopping – in this case, buying us lots of things for the new baby. We leave John in PC World (so he can stare dully at laptop specifications) and Chelsea in Starbucks (so she can drink lattes and get Wi-Fi on her mobile phone). We arrange to meet them in three hours outside Next (where my mum will have her final blow-out – buying something for everyone).

Meanwhile, we go inside every baby shop we come across and visit the baby sections in all the big department stores. Me and Lyd both hate shopping (and it's the last thing she wants to do whilst she's pregnant) but we put a brave face on because it's a good chance to communicate with my mum whilst she's in her element.

"So, what have Lydia's parents bought you?" Mum asks, as she looks at overpriced wooden toys in a shop called E is for Elephant.

"Nothing yet," I say.

"*Nothing?*"

"No, I don't think so."

"Nothing? Lydia? Is that right?"

"No, they never take us shopping. Do they, Vince?"

I shake my head with a smile. Lyd is great with my mum.

"Well, we'll have to fix that, won't we? You'll be needing all sorts."

Mum is full of provider's pride now, and on a shopping mission that only a veteran shopper of her standing can

62

complete within three hours. She rushes us to a more standardised baby shop and zooms around it.

"Going to need one of them, definitely one of them, one of those... that's nice... and one of these..."

We fail to keep pace with her and end up standing by a play area where toddlers are grabbing at an oversized abacus and some giant square cushions that double as building blocks. We stare at the children playing, mildly depressed.

"Charlie would have been six now," says Lyd. "You forget they keep growing, don't you?"

I take her hand.

When Mum finds us again she's managed to attain a trolley. I haven't seen anybody else with a trolley. God knows where she found it. She's filled it with all manner of products. At a glance it seems to be a mixture of bare essentials and completely superfluous tat.

"Mum. That's way too much. We don't need all that."

"Nonsense. This is just essentials."

"How is this essential?"

I pick up a tacky-looking blue teddy bear.

"Weeeell, they all need a teddy. Show me one baby without a teddy."

"It's too much, Mum. You can't afford all this."

"I can afford what I want to afford and don't think I'm done affording things yet."

Me and Lyd look at each other and smile with affection.

"We appreciate it, Linnie," says Lyd. "But he's right. It's too much. Besides, we've still got a lot of this kind of stuff up in the attic... from before."

My mum's face sinks.

"Oh, yes. I'm not thinking, am I? I'm not thinking at all. I'm thinking it's your first. But it's not, is it? Oh dear. I'm sorry, loves. I just didn't think."

"Mum, it's okay."

She's tearing up.

"You're just going to have to take out what you've already got. God, I'm sorry. I just didn't think."

Lyd goes to the trolley feigning a deeper interest than she actually has.

"It is lovely stuff you get here though, isn't it?" she says. "And it's nice to have *some* new."

My mum's face immediately reverts from sad to excited.

"That's what I say. It's nice to have some new, isn't it? And it is lovely stuff." She grabs Lyd's elbow and pulls her away. "Come and have a look at this comforter. It's a bit much but…"

I'm left waiting with the trolley.

In the evening Lyd gets out some takeaway menus and suggests we order a couple of large pizzas and eat them with the salad she made earlier. This idea sinks into the abyss without even being acknowledged. She puts the menus down on the coffee table and looks around to see what's wrong.

"What you getting?" Chelsea casually asks John, picking up the menu she deems appropriate, making sure Lyd knows that her salad idea has been derailed without debate.

When the menu has been passed around I order for us all. John: stuffed-crust mighty meaty. Mum: medium Hawaiian. Chelsea: stuffed-crust double pepperoni. Lyd: medium vegetarian. Me: medium Mexican chicken. Then there are the obligatory extras: garlic bread, dough balls, chicken dippers and stuffed jalapenos.

While we're waiting for it to arrive we let Chelsea run loose with the remote control, signing us up for a "TV and film on-demand" service. It's the only time she speaks with any enthusiasm to any of us about anything all day. My mum looks at me and Lyd sweetly, thanking us for making her so happy, which makes us both despair about the girl, but we both smile back awkwardly.

When the pizza comes my mum rushes to the door to pay.

Chelsea chooses the first film; a terrible coming-of-age comedy about a bunch of Californian girls with way too much of everything in their lives – like *Clueless* but without the irony. John chooses the second; an inane thriller set in Boston about a financially motivated kidnapping gone wrong.

Both films are put together well enough to hold their own but the plots and characters are pitifully transparent. That seems to be part of the fun though. Chelsea, in particular, likes pointing out (in a semi-aggressive fashion) who is going to do what and how they are going to end up.

"She's going to be the popular one at the end."

"They'll break up and he'll get off with her."

"She'll escape with him."

"It'll be him fighting him at the end."

When all our pizzas are finished my mum pulls out a bag of chocolate that she's brought from home and passes different bits around until at least a kilogram of sugar disappears into the spaces between the seemingly indigestible lumps of dough in our bellies. Throughout the night Chelsea gulps down a litre and a half of Coke, John empties six cans of bitter, my mum drinks four cups of tea and me and Lyd have a glass of Coke and a couple of teas.

By the end of the evening me and Lyd have terrible stomach aches and they seem to interpret this as a metropolitan softness and laugh at us. They're not suffering in the same way and instead give heavy sighs and stifled burps that seem to signify deep pleasure.

I've got through the day without any weirdness but, today more than ever, I've noticed that all three of my family members constantly deflect emotional contact. They hardly ever look people in the eye and rarely talk about anything except the things they want. It doesn't seem a particularly healthy way to behave but it does create space for your own anxieties to float around freely, ungazed upon. When we say goodnight I realise that it hasn't been a stressful day.

An hour later, staring at an all-too-familiar watermark on the ceiling, I'm hoping that tonight's wakefulness might be caffeine-related or due to the fact that I'm uncomfortably full. Maybe I'll start getting drowsy after an hour or so. But the tiredness doesn't come. Feelings of hopelessness sweep through me instead.

The sight of Lyd sleeping by my side, growing a human being in her womb, fills me with guilt. Pregnancy is a real risk to her body and it will change the shape of her bones for ever. Meanwhile, I'm betraying her, taking a needless risk – skipping my lithium every day – and all in the name of rediscovering a version of myself that might not have even existed in the first place. Crushing that pink pill and rinsing it down the sink is just part of my daily routine now. It makes me a liar, a coward, a fool. Why do I even imagine that I deserve a life with her?

I don't know what day it is, what time, what year. I'm not thinking like that. My sleep has been broken at least four times. Yesterday and tomorrow are islands I'm swimming between. My brain is pulsing. I can hear the beat of blood between my ear and the pillow. The darkness is an alien blue. There's a cold sweat on my back. A distant noise sounds on the edge of my senses, pulling me further into a waking state.

A mouse in the walls?

I sit up and sigh, reaching for the glass of water on my bedside table. I drink half of it and decide to relieve my bladder. Sometimes, even if I don't need to, squeezing out a few drops of urine is enough to convince myself that I've only woken up because I needed the toilet. Afterwards, getting back to sleep is the obvious next step. I have to avoid thoughts like, *Waking in the middle of the night is a symptom of the manic cycle*. I have to think stealthily.

I hear it again whilst I'm in the hallway, something shuffling somewhere. It's an animal of some kind. It lacks the inane lifelessness of a house noise. I stop on the spot and listen quietly, poised, my perceptions soaring.

There it is again.

It has a distinct direction. It's coming from Charlie's room. I move towards the doorway. As my hand hovers over the doorknob it begins to shake. I'm looking at my vibrating hand but it doesn't seem like my hand. I can't feel the shaking. I can only see it.

Another sound.

Above me this time.

Something scurrying in the attic. I rub my arm up and down and listen carefully but the noises seem to have stopped. The tremors in my right hand are settling down. The feeling is returning to my extremities.

I begin to picture Lyd catching me standing in the hallway in the middle of the night, lurking by Charlie's door, and I suddenly remember that it's not Charlie's door, my mum and John are in there. Chelsea is downstairs on the couch. Charlie doesn't exist. I feel disorientated, aggrieved. It's been a long time since I've had to realise that he's dead. It used to happen every morning. This time it was smaller, less intense, but it was there.

I go to the bathroom and then head back to bed.

We planned to take my family for a walk on the Heath, let them stare down at London from Parliament Hill and bring them back for a healthy lunch before sending them on their way, but they all stay in bed until 11am. Chelsea goes upstairs to shower and then Mum and John come down with their bags packed. I offer them breakfast, drinks, anything, but they're set to go.

"Chelsea wants McDonald's," is all Mum says, clearly a little bit upset.

On the doorstep Mum comes up close and sneaks fifty pounds into my hand.

"No," I say, trying to give it back. "You already bought too much yesterday."

She tenses her teeth and widens her eyes, begging me not

to draw Chelsea or John's attention to it, then clasps my hand around it.

"It's for that *demanding TV* thing. You didn't have to do that. It made her night, that did."

"I'm far too old for this," I whisper in protest.

"You're never too old for a treat from your mum."

She kisses my cheek and then pinches it and wobbles the flesh around with a wink.

Getting into their car, Chelsea looks over at us, sizes us up, almost says something that looks like it could have been a compliment, sort of nods and then climbs in. John starts the engine and raises a dull salute. My mum gives Lyd an intense hug.

"Look after him, won't you, love?"

"I will, Linnie," she says.

Mum comes back to me and squeezes her arms around me.

"And you look after her."

"I will," I say.

"And at least think about getting a proper job, so you can take her out and buy her something nice."

"Okay, Mum. I'll think about it."

After they drive away, I stumble into the kitchen, lean on the counter and begin despondently eating grapes from the fruit bowl.

"That wasn't too bad, was it?" says Lyd, following me in and quickly clearing up the last traces of having had guests.

"No, I guess not."

"What's up?"

"Nothing. I'm just being dramatic."

"Go on."

"I don't know. It's just that I really want to be able to connect with her, but we never quite manage it."

"She seemed to have a nice time?"

"I know. Like I said, I'm being dramatic. I didn't sleep well. After I see her I can never quite shake this feeling that neither of us was really there. We try to reach each other but we can't."

"That's sad, honey. But everything seemed fine to me."

"Maybe I just want too much."

"I don't understand," says Lyd. "What isn't there?"

"Feelings, I guess. They're there, but they're behind glass. We can see them in each other but we just can't feel them."

"Your childhood was quite complicated."

"I just wish we got more out of it. And I wish those two would respect her a little bit more, see how lucky they are to have her."

"I'm sure they do… People can't go around feeling things and expressing things all the time."

"No. I know. But they're so *cold* with each other. It scares me that families can be that way. They're all so separate. They don't even know they're depressed."

Lyd finally understands.

"It's okay," she says, coming to me and wrapping her arms around my shoulders. "Our family will be nothing like that."

This is the first time Lyd has referred to the future in a positive way since we found out she was pregnant. It's the first time she's held me since I packed up Charlie's room. I grab onto her. I don't want the moment to end.

FIVE

The Green Man, one of folklore's oldest gatekeepers, is said to present his face in leaves and foliage. Those who see him before they enter a wood must beware the tricks he might play. His summer trees are catchers of light and beneath his green skin is a daytime twilight and a starless night of the truest dark. Though the gateway his face creates is impassable, and investigation reveals only dissolution, time spent in his shadows can unearth portions of his world beyond. He is sometimes said to send out woodland creatures to give obscure messages or play pranks and it has also been told that, on very rare occasions, he can blow the entire spirit of the natural world right through a person and shake them to the very core of their being.

On my computer screen this morning there was a yellow Post-It note: *Call Sergio*. I first met Sergio living in a shared house in Hackney after university. He was having trouble finding a decent job and I was unemployed and struggling with my writing so we became daytime dependents, meeting up in the kitchen for chats and cups of tea. Despite being vastly different we formed a bond that mattered to both of us so, even when he became a wealthy business lawyer and I remained a destitute writer, we stayed in regular contact.

When Lyd got close with Sergio's wife, Gloria, we mostly started seeing each other as a group of four. Lots of couples become friends because their children are similar ages, or they have a similar income and like to do similar things. We got on well despite our differences. They are second generation British-Spanish, much richer than us, unable to have children and completely uninterested in literature or science. Yet, somehow, it worked from the outset. We always had good times together.

When Charlie arrived we didn't pull towards other couples with children and they didn't pull away as a couple who couldn't have children. Me and Lyd were insistent that parenthood wasn't going to define us as completely as it did for others and Sergio and Gloria enjoyed the proximity to Charlie. The five of us were like an extended family. They babysat for us all the time. In some ways, they got to take on the portion of the parenting identity that we didn't want and they couldn't have. When Charlie died they were devastated and that kept us tight, even through the dark times.

When I see Sergio, he's walking towards the entrance of the café/bar where we always meet. He, or I, would usually just wait at the table. He's wearing a designer polo shirt, beige chinos and brown, tasselled moccasins; the usual preppy stuff that I constantly mock him about.

"Long time, buddy."

He offers me his hand with an intense smile.

"Good to see you," I say.

But this handshake is slightly too formal. We usually hug.

He glances over his shoulder nervously. He seems a little bit hyper. I'm now working on the assumption that this meeting is a set up. I'm about to be analysed in some horrible, probing way.

"There's someone I want you to meet," he says.

This could be worse than I expected.

A shrink?

An intervention?

I follow him, scanning all the tables. There's no one I can imagine we're going to end up sitting with. The person we're heading towards makes the least sense of all: a teenage Japanese girl with large breasts and a surly glare.

Sergio sits down beside her and proudly puts his arm around her shoulders in a possessive and sexually satisfied way. His smile is beaming. She seems underwhelmed. I sit down apprehensively. This isn't about me at all.

"This is Mitsu," he says. "Mitsu, Vince."

I was wrong about her age. Now that I'm up close, she looks to be in her mid-twenties. Her face is stubborn and gloomy. It was her schoolgirl look that threw me off: crisp white blouse, black cardigan, pleated grey skirt, white ankle socks with frilled edges and flat-bottomed patent leather shoes with a strap. Three of her blouse buttons are undone, revealing the wispy edges of what must be an enormous tattoo that creeps up onto her cleavage from all directions.

"Hi," I say, offering my hand.

She reaches for it limply, barely makes contact and is seemingly appalled by the formality of the gesture. She has the vacant disinterest of an extreme masochist and radiates emotional trauma. I smile awkwardly and look back at Sergio.

"I'm in love," he says.

Mitsu looks at him disapprovingly.

"So I see," I say. "When did, *this* happen?"

Unable to bear hearing what Sergio is about to say, Mitsu slides off her chair and walks towards the toilets. I can't help but watch her walk away. Her nonchalance, alongside the thinly veiled sexual statement her clothing makes, is hard for the libido to ignore. Every man in the place watches her lustily, even the family orientated proprietor at the cash desk. I notice that she has the word *December* tattooed in red ink on the back of her right calf.

"*December*?" I ask.

"Isn't she amazing?" he says, shrugging.

"What's going on, Serge?"

He tries to compose his face, project some seriousness, or empathy, but he is full of lust for his overgrown schoolgirl.

72

"I know," he says, unable to control the glee creeping onto his face. He takes a breath and tries again. "I know."

"Does she know?"

"That I'm married?"

"No. Does Gloria know?"

"I've left her," he says, pausing for a second before asserting himself with a single nod.

"When?"

"This morning… I've never felt like this, Vince. She blows my mind." He looks over his shoulder. "She does anything I say. *An-y-thing*."

"Please," I say, holding a hand out for him to stop.

"You should hear some of things that come out of her mouth. She's from a different world."

He smiles, shrugging again.

"And Gloria?"

"I've never felt like this… It's passion. Real passion."

"Is Gloria okay?"

"Gloria?"

"Yes. *Gloria*."

"She doesn't know. Not yet."

"Doesn't know what?"

"Well, anything… But I can't go back there, Vince. That life is over. It's done."

"Okay. Okay. Stop. Do you realise what you sound like?"

A flash of resentment passes across his face but is quickly displaced by joy.

"I don't expect you to understand."

"What *do* you expect?"

He glances over to the toilets.

"I need you to tell Gloria for me."

"*What*?" I say, standing up, intuitively beginning to leave.

He jumps up, runs around the table and stands in front of me. He has somehow grabbed a white envelope during these quick movements and now holds it in front of him.

"Please. Just give her this."

"No way. I'm not implicating myself in this," I say. "She'll think I knew."

"The letter explains everything."

"So? Drop it through the letter box."

"She deserves more than that."

"No shit," I say, laughing with disbelief. "You've been married eight years."

"But no kids," he adds, with a half-smile, as if this is a saving grace.

"Lyd said you'd been accusing *her* of cheating."

"She's been at it for months. Trust me. I know she has."

"No. I'm not getting involved in this. You can talk to her yourself."

"I *can't*," he says, his smile beaming for a split second as he sees Mitsu exiting the toilet. His expression is suddenly urgent. "Mitsu says it has to be gung-ho, just the two of us, no turning back, Bonnie and Clyde, Micky and Mallory, you know?"

"You're married. She's… I don't know what she is."

"I know. I know. But you're the only person I can ask. *Please*."

He looks her way again and desperately forces the envelope onto my chest. I shake my head, fold the envelope and put it in my pocket. He mouths *Thank you*, and tries to insist that I sit back down as she slouches onto her seat. I refuse but I'm still too intrigued to leave.

"How did you two meet?" I ask, standing by the table.

"Casino," says Mitsu, lethargic, a slight accent.

"You're not gambling again?" I ask Sergio.

"Not anymore."

"When was that?"

"Three weeks ago," says Mitsu, bored.

"Three weeks. And now you're… Jesus… I should go… Sorry, Mitsu. Something came up whilst you were… in there."

74

She does not acknowledge this. Sergio jumps up and follows me for a couple of steps.

"Thanks for this, Vince," he whispers, patting my shoulder.

"Yeah," I say, walking away.

I step up to Sergio and Gloria's house and ring the doorbell. Gloria answers in a frilly black negligée, stockings and a silk robe that is open and hanging by her sides. Her face is heavily made up. The sight of her breasts bulging and her curvy thighs pinched by the stockings is a complete surprise to me. Up until recently, this would have been completely out of character. When me and Sergio get drunk together, he sometimes whinges about their sex life; how she never goes down on him, how their sex can never just be about fun or fucking, how there's too much inhibition and emotional preciousness, how, unprovoked, during bedroom conversations, she needlessly lectures him about her refusal to be "a man's prize", or about sex not being a fantasy of power and worship. These are not the irks of a man whose wife has an outfit like this.

Seeing me, the initial sexual confidence drains from her face, her spine slouches and she quickly closes her robe and ties it up.

"What are you doing here?" she asks, poking her head out the doorway, looking both ways and then grabbing my arm and dragging me inside. "You're going to have to be quick."

"Jesus, Gloria."

"What?" she asks, impatiently. "What?"

"Nothing. It doesn't matter."

She slants her head at me as a warning.

"What is it? Dinner? The four of us some time? Message for Serge? Something from Lydia? What?"

I take the envelope out of my pocket.

"Message *from* Serge," I correct her.

"Fine, fine," she says, snapping it out of my hand, barely recognising the irregularity of this. "Go. Go."

"Okay," I say. "I just want you to know, I didn't know anything about it until this morning."

It now dawns on her that this situation is strange. She closes the door with a confused expression, glances at me critically and then opens the letter. Reading it, her frenetic energy depletes in seconds. By the time she's turned the first page she is sitting at the bottom of the stairs barely able to keep her head above her shoulders.

The letter is long. As she is reading the final page the doorbell rings. Gloria looks up with a dumbfounded expression, as though she's not sure what the noise signifies. Her eye make-up has run down her cheeks. Her crying has been silent.

"I'll get rid of them," I say.

"No!" she shouts, suddenly coming into herself.

She panics, flings the letter aside and runs towards me.

Bemused, I look through the clouded pane of glass by the side of the front door and see the blur of a familiar figure that I can't quite place.

"No!" repeats Gloria, trying to forbid me to even look.

She stands in front of the door and pushes me away. Intrigued, and fairly certain that I know the person outside, I try to reach around Gloria's waist for the door handle but she thrusts her breasts out at me, forcing me to take a step back and desist.

"Don't," she says, serious, broadening her stance.

To my horror she seems to be implying that there could be an accusation of assault in store for me. She's desperate.

The doorbell rings again, twice in quick succession, and is followed by immediate, heavy knocking.

"Gloria? I can hear you. What's going on?"

The voice is muffled. The identity of this person is dangling just out of reach, it won't come to me, but Gloria sighs, her protective stance slumps, and, presuming that the game is now up, she opens the door.

Peter, Lyd's big brother, is standing in the doorway in

a Prada suit, holding a chilled bottle of Cristal. His face does not falter from its relaxed, overconfident smile when he sees me.

"Alright, Vince? What are you doing here?"

Back home, sitting in a chair on the patio after a late lunch, my feet up on the round outdoor table, I can barely stay awake. The stress of the morning was exhausting. Gloria and Peter have forced me into a corner, making me swear that I won't tell Lyd about them. I hate lying to her. I'm deceiving her enough as it is. The hope of getting things back to our usual open and honest state is the only thing keeping me on course. Another secret feels like too much, a step too far.

I'm also worried about what Sergio and Gloria are doing to each other and, even though it is a relatively small aspect of the situation, I feel personally betrayed by their lack of regard for the friendship the four of us share. There was a time when we could sit around this outdoor table without a negative thought crossing between us. With these affairs, those days are gone. They've thrown what we had away.

I try to think about writing to distract myself from the pressure of all these lies and betrayals. There's a quote on a Post-It that I've stuck on my desk that's been working its way into the story. Something Kant wrote. It's slowly becoming a theme in the work, connecting the different narratives.

On the great map of the spirit only a few points are illuminated.

I say it to myself a few times, trying to mull on how it relates to the fictional events, how I can make it resonate, but I can't concentrate on concepts or imaginary people. The sun is shining and, today, after Mitsu, after Peter, brightness is enough.

Next door's cherry blossoms are blooming; glorious pinks and whites. The sunlight makes them look unreal, blurring all the edges with the intense purity of their colour, creating clouds of candy floss and marshmallows.

My eyes keep giving in to sleep. My head lolls, dips, and then jerks up, awake. I do this again and again and, between the snoozes, through the cracks, the colours of the trees gleam. Each time I slip away it's for a little while longer. It starts with a second, two seconds, four, gradually moves up to a minute. Somewhere along the way I'm unconscious long enough to call it sleep. Five minutes. Ten minutes. I start waking with my chin on my collarbone and a crick in my neck. Finally, I sleep for so long that I lose track of time altogether.

A dull strain in my ankle wakes me. I open my eyes and see that Blackie is standing on the tip of my right foot, sideways, in profile, his black left eye with its golden ring piercing me intensely. His shiny yellow beak is glistening in the sun, clouds of pink-and-white blossom pulsate behind him. This is the first time he has come to me since I annoyed him over a week ago. It's the first time he's ever come to me without my coaxing him with sultanas.

He stands in silence. He's not here for food. He is here to show me his true self. But he is extremely disappointed in me. After seeking and gaining his trust, and making him a part of my journey to a new self, I showed him off like a trained pet. He must gaze into me and see if I have the conviction and integrity to see my journey through. I'm not sure how he tells me all this. It is implicit.

He jumps, turns one hundred and eighty degrees and faces the opposite direction, still on my foot, looking at me with his other eye. Uneasiness rises in me. Showing me his profile like this is a demonstration of his power. He is turning himself into a symbol, a pure being, and by doing so he is opening a chasm into another realm. Behind him, in the amorphous pinks and whites, there is an ancient world, older than I can imagine, and he is one of its messengers.

He jumps again, this time he lands facing me. His eyes contain the unflinching supremacy of nature. There is no compassion in their black depths. He sees me for exactly what I am. I feel deep and sincere shame and this shame forms a bridge between us, connects us. His beak opens and, as I look down his throat, something, an idea, a message, pours out from inside him, from beyond him:

I will save you if you try with all your heart. I will protect you. But if you are weak, I will leave you to be devoured. I will stand aside as your world falls apart.

"I'll try," I whisper. "With all my heart."

My eyes are closed. I'm not sure how long I've been asleep. The entire blackbird experience could have been a dream but when I open my eyes I find myself face down on the lawn. My head is throbbing. I have no idea how I got here.

Blackie is standing in profile about a metre away from me on the grass. He jumps one hundred and eighty degrees and my headache calms slightly. He jumps one hundred and eighty degrees again and I feel almost normal, as though nothing has happened. He is just a bird on my lawn.

– *chink-chink, chook-chook, chink-chink, chook-chook* –
(*Goodbye.*)
He flies away.

SIX

Human beings have three types of photoreceptor in their retinas: red, green and blue. This is the reason they see the range of colours that they do. Their spherical eyes are only able to focus on one thing at a time, changing the way they perceive, understand and interact with reality. Birds, on the other hand, have four photoreceptors and their cones' maximal absorption peaks are higher, enabling them to see ultraviolet light and countless additional variants of colour. Their eyes are also flatter so they can focus on lots of things at once. However, the unfathomable difference is the fourth cone. Birds see a whole field of visual information that is beyond human comprehension. People can try to guess what it is by studying the behaviours and attributes of birds (some experts say polarised light, others magnetic fields) but in the end they have to accept the limitations of the imagination and admit that birds can see an entire dimension that people are unable to envision.

I wake up at around 5:30am and decide to get up and make Lyd breakfast: orange juice, porridge with seeds and sliced dates, coffee, toast with butter and honey – a basic but broad weekday breakfast. I listen to Lucille Bogan as I prepare it.

After showering, Lyd arrives in the kitchen wearing her white robe. The idea of me eating into the few private minutes she has in her day annoys her at first. She relaxes when she sees the breakfast laid out for her and even more when I turn my music off.

"I won't have time to eat all this," she says, almost apologetically, running her fingers through her hair to distribute whatever product she puts in whilst it's still wet. "I've got a big day."

I approach her.

"I know," I say, reaching for her waist. "I just wanted to treat you."

She lifts an eyebrow and registers how tired I look.

"What are you doing up at this time anyway?"

"Just woke up," I say, reaching for the knot at the front of her robe.

She flattens my hands to her stomach.

"I usually just grab an apple," she says.

"You should be eating properly. All the critical growth happens around this time. Organs, all that stuff."

She's amused that I know more about her pregnancy than she does.

"*Really*?"

"Really." I submit to her amusement with a smile. "I've been reading up."

I slide my hands from under hers, around her hips and down her robe until I'm touching the skin of her lower thighs. At the first indication of upwards movement, she takes a step back and looks at me with a playful warning.

"We don't want to interrupt the critical growth, do we?"

I move away with a half-amused, half-rejected smile, wondering when we last had sex. My libido is pointlessly blazing. It has been for days. Lyd walks over to the breakfast counter and pulls herself onto a stool with a sigh.

"You not eating?" she asks, skipping the porridge and spreading honey on a piece of toast, no butter.

"Too early," I say, patting my stomach.

"For you or your little friend?"

She drinks half of her orange juice, whipping an amused glance at me.

"He doesn't come anymore."

She glances again, this time with a frown, but quickly dispels the need to worry. She begins eating her slice of toast.

"Oh well," she says. "I'm surprised he kept it up for as long as he did. Maybe he got bored of sultanas?"

"Maybe," I say.

It doesn't occur to her that I would lie about the importance of Blackie's role in my life, or that my heart might be racing at the mere mention of him.

"He'll probably come back," she offers, but with a tone that suggests that it's unimportant either way. "Creatures and habits and all that."

"It doesn't matter," I say, fighting the blood gushing through my veins, attempting to project an image of normality. "It's mating season. I think he's paired off."

She looks out through the patio doors as though she's only just registered that it's spring. The brightness makes her wince.

"You okay?"

"Just another headache," she says.

"Can I get you anything for it?"

She shakes her head, puts her elbow on the breakfast counter and clamps her middle finger and thumb around her temples, moving them in tiny circles. With the other hand, she pushes her plate away. I start clearing up.

When Lyd leaves the house it feels empty and I'm uninspired, almost afraid of writing. Words seem to have abandoned me. I stare at a blank page in my notebook and then check my email.

The inbox is full of the usual stuff from websites I'm signed up to – books I should read, music I should hear, tickets I should buy, films I should watch, jobs I should apply for, clothes I should wear, old web accounts I should tend to, competitions I should enter, food I should order, discounts I should take advantage of – an algorithmic world scarily close to correct but, thankfully, just slightly wrong. There's nothing from the magazines I sent the last batch of short stories to, nothing from old friends, nothing from an actual person.

I check my junk mail.

It's even worse in there: offensively transparent scams and corporate click-bait that even my corporate email provider thinks is too invasive. I'm careful with my email address so it took them fifteen years but the Viagra spam I've heard so much about has finally started arriving. In amongst the devious titles designed to get me to click there's:

From: *CHARLIE*

Subject: (1) Re: contact me please…

I delete it along with all the rest of the junk.

When I click back on my inbox my junk folder has (1) next to it. I click it and look.

Email from: *CHARLIE*

Subject: (2) Re: contact me please…

I click delete again and it pops back into my junk inbox, instantly this time.

Email from: *CHARLIE*

Subject: (3) Re: contact me please…

I start deleting it again and again until my head falls into a spiral. When I stop clicking it says:

Email from: *CHARLIE*

Subject: (56) Re: contact me please…

It must be a clever new kind of junk mail, a tracker in it or something. I'm not technologically gifted but I know better than to open it.

The word CHARLIE flashing back onto my screen again and again has made me feel like he's in the house somewhere. Behind me. Around me. I need to get out, see a fresh face; somebody separate from the entanglements of my intimate life but close enough to understand them. The only person who fits into this category is Jamal. I stand up impulsively and leave, heading towards him.

I don't see a single blackbird on the twenty-minute walk over to his house but I can hear them everywhere; hiding in bushes, behind houses, in trees. My knock on the door is slightly desperate, like I need to escape the noise.

Jamal answers the door with an unlit joint hanging out of his mouth, squints at outside's brightest and motions for me to follow him inside. His long, greying dark hair is held back in a ponytail. He's wearing his usual black T-shirt and ripped, oil-stained jeans. As always, the entire floor of his house is lined with newspaper and covered with small chunks of steel and aluminium that have neat lines of washers, pieces of plastic and nuts and bolts next to them. It smells of spray oil, tar and cannabis resin. There are carefully exposed foot-shaped holes in the newspaper to indicate how people must navigate the room. The couch, the chairs, the coffee table and the kitchen table (from a sideways glance) are all covered with newspapers and motor parts. Each stair has a carburettor sitting on a newspaper, pushed over to the right-hand side.

Upstairs there are two bedrooms. He uses one as a workshop, for more serious work, but his actual bedroom is where he spends most of his time, polishing pieces of metal cross-legged on his bed and putting things together so he can sell them on the Internet and make his meagre living (he inherited his house from a childless, divorced aunty who always favoured him over her other nieces and nephews).

A quick look into his bathroom reveals a bathtub full of engine parts soaking in a murky grey liquid which is giving off noxious fumes. I fleetingly wonder how he cleans himself but realise I haven't seen him without oil-stained skin for almost ten years. I'm not sure he does wash.

In his bedroom, he carefully takes the four corners of a newspaper, gathers up the pieces of a camshaft and puts the bundle in the foot of his wardrobe, revealing an old wooden chair for me to sit on in the process. He steps up onto his bed as though navigating the ledge of a fifty-storey building (there are lots of loose pieces of metal on sheets of newspaper) and gestures towards the chair. By the time I get to it and sit down he has relit his slightly oil-stained joint and is scraping rust from the main section of a crankshaft.

Until now Jamal has been silent. He can only talk properly whilst he works. He's better at engaging when his mind is diverted.

"So," he says, "what can I do for you?"

"Just needed to get out of the house."

"Spliff?"

He offers it to me and glances at my legs, jigging up and down.

"No, thanks," I say, putting my hands on my thighs to stop them moving. "Feeling a bit edgy as it is."

"Yeah? What's going on?"

"Nothing. The usual. Life stuff." I stand up and walk over to the window, evading little piles of scrap on the floor. "Do you know Serge and Gloria are cheating on each other?"

I met Jamal in the same shared house as the one I lived in with Sergio after university. Whilst Sergio was seeing Gloria in the evenings, we often smoked weed and had long philosophical discussions. Jamal and Sergio share a passion for vintage cars so they always stayed in touch a little bit. Occasionally, they go to a motor show or trade fair together. I sometimes think they keep it up because I'm an umbilical cord between them – this could be sheer narcissism though.

"It was always going to happen," he says.

"You think?"

"Yeah, man. She constantly forces her presence everywhere in his life, undermines him in front of his friends, emasculates him. He'll be having a fling with someone who lets him cut loose a bit, most likely younger. And Gloria's probably realised that she bullies Serge so much because she wants someone more macho, someone who won't put up with all her oppressive shit."

"Do me a favour. Never tell me what you think about me and Lyd."

He laughs at this, but he's also frowning at the way I've started treading back and forth across his room. I can't help it though. I can't stay still.

"You two are a good match. Yin and yang. And probably not the way around you imagine."

"Maybe. And you're bang on. Serge *is* running off with someone younger. East Asian girl. I guess he's cutting loose but, in some ways, she seemed to have him by the balls too. Gloria's been sleeping with Peter."

"Peter, Peter? Peter Bateman, Peter?"

"Yep. The psycho himself."

Jamal shakes his head and scrubs with more ferocity.

"Is there anyone that guy doesn't end up fucking? He truly doesn't know where to draw the line."

(Peter once seduced and had sex with Jamal's little sister in Serge and Gloria's downstairs bathroom when she was drunk at their summer barbeque.)

"I try not to think about it," I say. "The world's depressing enough without wondering why all intelligent and beautiful women seem to want to sleep with him."

"Does Lydia know?"

"No. Not yet. I told them I wouldn't say anything but I can't keep lying to her. With Lyd, it's like the truth is always there, talking to her, even if I'm not saying anything. It starts twittering in my ears. The only upside is that she's pregnant, and I don't want to upset her. So at least there's actually a reason to keep quiet."

He raises his eyebrows and stops scraping at his metal.

"Lydia's pregnant?"

"Yeah."

"You can't just slip the P-bomb in like that. Pregnant?"

"Yes. Pregnant."

"This is major, life-altering news, man. No wonder you're treading the boards like a caged tiger... Unless you're trying to talk it down? Is that what you're doing? Do you not want to talk about it?"

He starts scraping again. I continue pacing between the far wall and window, careful not to step on any motor parts.

"I don't mind," I say. "But I think I might be unravelling a bit. Not because of the pregnancy. Well, maybe. I don't know."

"So you've come to your guru for some sage advice."

"You wish you were my guru."

He smiles.

"Congratulations, by the way."

"Thanks," I say. "I think it could be good for us."

"So what's *unravelling*?"

I peer out the window. There's a blackbird pecking for worms down on a bare patch of the mostly overgrown lawn.

"Oh, nothing really," I say, with an overwhelming and slightly frightening intuition that I'm not allowed to tell him about Blackie now that I've seen this blackbird. "Nothing specific."

The blackbird flies up into a tree. I feel a pang of relief and turn to face Jamal. He sucks on his joint a couple of times and puts it back in his ashtray, confused. I have to tell him something.

"I stopped taking my lithium when I found out about the pregnancy."

This statement earns me a rare second of eye contact.

"Good for you, man," he says, nodding and then looking back down at his crankshaft. "That's great. What does Lyd think about it?"

"She doesn't know."

"So that's the real secret. Not this stuff with Peter."

"I just didn't want to be... I don't know."

"I never thought you should have been put on that stuff in the first place. You know how I feel about people medicating trauma and depression. All that chemical balance bullshit."

"Ironic given your lifestyle choice."

He lifts up his joint and smiles at it.

"Hey, I'm not depressed, man. This stuff just helps me think straight. Most men need a woman. I need this. I thought you'd lost a couple of pounds."

"Really?"

"You look less bloated. More like you. Do you want some chai?"

"Sure."

He gets up and leaves the room, grabbing a darkly stained mug on the way.

I look around with a sigh. The room, and the impossibility of a woman spending the night in it, make me feel momentarily sorry for him but I also empathise with the level of solitude he has sought out. On the surface it might seem like the house of a disturbed kleptomaniac but it's also the systematic domain of a cleverly integrated and highly functioning recluse. There is strength and self-assurance in the environment, motivation and attainment. In his presence, I never feel pity or concern. In fact, I envy his resolve. It is only when he leaves the room that the loneliness of it creeps over me. And that is my loneliness, not his.

He comes back with two cups of chai, strong and black. I take mine with a nod and he carefully gets back into his cross-legged position on the bed. He takes a sip, leans over and puts the cup on his bedside table (which is covered with miscellaneous washers and nuts and bolts). He picks up a small, curved toothbrush with metal bristles and gets back to scraping and scrubbing his crankshaft.

"I'm so glad you're off that shit," he says. "It was no good for you."

I nod in agreement, quickly, anxiously.

"If she finds out though..." I say, pausing with dread. "And, I mean, I can barely sit still. I'm awake all night. I feel like I've got electricity running through my veins."

"But that can't last, can it? That's not how you used to feel, before?"

"I don't think so. It can't be. But if she finds out..."

He pauses and takes a look at me, wondering if anybody could see anything but a nervous wreck. He doesn't seem to decide either way but he's excellent at concealing his thoughts when he wants to be.

"How's the queen of the subatomic dealing with being pregnant?" he asks, deciding to balance his view of the situation with an interpretation of Lyd's current state.

"She's busy. Working all the time, as ever. I think she might be drinking too much. Well, for someone who's, you know. But I can't really get a handle on her. At the start it seemed okay. She seemed to be working it out. She's gone more distant now. I thought I'd got through to her a few weeks back but I've started getting the feeling she's not really there again."

"Sounds about right. She's always been evasive. She likes to work things out on her own. But she always seems to get there in the end. She always comes back to you."

I nod, fearing the hope he's trying to give me.

Jamal always has a pragmatic and assured tone of voice. His words come out spoken as singular truths. More often than not, he's extremely objective and insightful but he occasionally misses the mark completely. This tone of his is part of the strength that comes from his solitude, because he never has to mediate his opinion or compromise for somebody else, but I've come to realise that I can't always trust it.

I watch him scraping at his metal, grateful for his friendship. All the things that soothe and satiate his being happen with mechanical precision; rolling joints, cleaning scrap, fitting things together, taking things apart. Everything is always straightforward with him. The world holds no secrets. All the parts fit together.

"And you're alright?" he asks. "The withdrawals aren't too bad? You're not seeing pink elephants or anything?"

"No, no," I say, looking out the window. "Just, you know, a bit anxious. A bit mental. Because I can't really show it."

He nods absently.

"Good. That's good, man. She can't say your heart's in the wrong place, can she? That's what I'm taking from this. I know how she feels about you towing the line, and why she wants it that way, but you don't want to be some kind of zombie-dad, do you?"

This is all I wanted, to hear somebody say that I'm doing the right thing, but part of me is appalled that he can say I'm on the right track.

"Thanks," I say. "But please don't tell anyone I'm off it."

"You know me better than that. You must think it's the right thing to do though, for the baby."

"I just need to get back to me."

"Cutting out the lithium has got to be the best way to go about it."

I nod and start pacing back and forth again, taking compulsive sips of my chai. I finish mine before he even reaches for his second sip. He's deeply engrossed in bringing the shine back to the surface of the curved hunk of steel he's holding. He eventually puts it down, lights his joint and reaches over for his cup.

"It's such a relief to tell somebody," I say.

"No wonder you're on edge, man, trying to keep something like this locked up."

"I hope you don't mind. I feel like I've just got to…"

I put my cup down on the windowsill and loosen my arms. I pivot on the balls of my feet, shake my hands and release a bizarre, nasal roar: "Uuuunnncchhhhrrrrrr." Jamal puts the end of his joint out in the ashtray, exhales with a grin and takes a big gulp of his chai.

"That's it," he says. "Wig out, man. Let it all hang loose."

I allow my arms to flop down and shake my body and head from side to side. Jamal laughs and starts making another joint.

"That feels good," I say. "I'm so coiled up."

"You've got to let out your weird, man."

"I really do."

I shake my face, bounce up and down and make more, strange guttural noises. Jamal is increasingly amused and impressed. He is the only person I know who I could behave this way in front of. A lot of the major decisions he has made in life have been due to his difference, and his fear of the normal. Moments like this only confirm the meaning of our friendship for us.

Feeling accepted for who and what I am, I dance further into my weirdness. My meat and bones begin to feel slack and loose. I jolt and jerk, twist and spasm. My body is a living concept, nebulous and unique. I'm a demented ballerina, an electric chicken. I'm thrashing and twirling, shaking and writhing, completely lost in the pleasure of it all.

When I finally stop, out of breath and pleased with myself, I notice that Jamal isn't smiling anymore. He's looking fixedly down at the fresh joint he's making, reluctant to raise his eyes. I can see the wilfulness in his refusal to glimpse my way.

My smile drops. I look at the floor. Somewhere along the way I've kicked one of his piles of scrap and scattered it across the floor, mixing it in with two other piles.

"Shit, sorry," I say, bending down, beginning to gather it up.

He pulls up his right cheek in a tense, forced smile and continues to look down at his joint.

I quickly pluck out the pieces of metal that look out of place, because they don't fit in any neat lines. But once I've gathered up all the obvious ones the piles become confusing. Lines of bolts appear in two directions at once, crossing each other. Everything looks increasingly random. There's no order. After moving a big piece of aluminium over to the kicked pile I begin to get anxious that I'm making things even worse, that I've completely shuffled the order of everything and it will be better if I just stop.

"I think I got it back how it was," I say, sitting back down on the wooden chair, knowing that there is no way that I've managed to put things back in their original place.

He gives the same nod and forced smile, looking at his joint.

I sigh and look towards the window. My legs are still and the anxiety has gone but it took too much. I went too far. There must be something wrong with me. Jamal is looking downwards too intensely. I think I'm going to leave.

SECOND
TRIMESTER

ONE

In June's warmer, longer days growth and replenishment replace the struggle to reproduce and survive. Food becomes abundant and rearing is in full swing. Poppies, orchids and foxgloves add blush to fields. Ducklings, goslings and cygnets waddle behind their parents. Grasshoppers and crickets begin to chirp in meadows. Butterfly wings unfurl and take flight. Dragonflies hover over water. Female bats suckle inch-long pups. House martins, swifts and swallows swoop and glide, diving for insects. Fawns fall and antlers rise. Baby badgers squint at their first night sky. Though much is lost or stolen, destroyed or killed, more is found and given, created and born. The rustling of life is everywhere.

We have the dating scan this afternoon so Lyd's taken the day off. I'm sitting at my desk pretending to write, realising (because of Lyd's presence in the house) that I haven't been working properly since Blackie messed with my mind in the back garden. I have six chapters, a whole bunch of scraps and no focus or momentum to put any of the rest of it together. Nothing correlates. All the chapters are about different people, in different times, in different places. I no longer have any idea what I'm working on.

Two weeks ago I used editing as an excuse to scroll down the same six chapters again and again. On the Friday I sent my first three chapters to my agent, Angela "not the dead novelist" Carter, and convinced myself that this was enough of an achievement for a week.

Last week, along with the pointless scrolling and unfocused rereading, I was checking my email for a response from her thirty, forty, fifty times a day. Constantly clicking, scrolling, clicking. She still hasn't got back to me.

Usually, when I send Angela pages, she at least acknowledges them. Later, she gets back to me with ideas about where we might send extracts for some advance publicity or else she suggests areas that could do with a little bit of tightening up. I'm beginning to think that she's so embarrassed by what I sent her that she's ignoring me.

I try to forget about it and instead focus on why I've ground to a halt. I revisit my archaeology metaphor where the unmapped charters of fiction are the entire landmass and the seed of inspiration, the excitement of the new thing, is like the first moment, after months of methodical digging, when the archaeologist reveals a small portion of an ancient bone. What follows – the real work, dusting away at the bones, following alien curves, revealing unforeseen crevices, allowing the hidden object to reveal itself – that's where I got lost.

I have to start again where I left off; that's what Lyd's presence in the house tells me. I need to reconnect with the bones, let them surprise me, trust that slowly following them will lead me further into their deeper structure. Their subterranean world is full of incomplete fragments but I have to believe in my initial feeling; that this is a special project, the different strands are part of a singular structure, I have to keep going and see it through.

The doorbell rings. A distraction. I rush down the stairs but Lyd's already there. She opens the door to her brother, Peter, whom she is extremely surprised to see.

"Oh. *Hi*. Did I tell you about the scan?"

"The what?"

"What are you doing here? Come in, come in."

"Vince…" he says, seeing me on the stairs and nodding, "erm, told me you'd be around. Did he not tell you I called?"

I make my way down the rest of the stairs. He looks at me with a pitiful need for me to corroborate his story. He did not call. He must be here to see me. He would have thought Lyd was at work. She turns her head to face me.

"Sorry. I forgot," I say.

Tension drifts out of both of their faces.

"Maybe he did mention the scan," Peter concedes, unusually generous. "I just remembered that you were going to be at home. I thought we could… eat."

He holds up a brown takeaway bag.

There's something different about him. He's sniffing a lot, which probably means he was snorting coke last night (hopefully not this morning), but it's not that. It's beneath that. His face has softened. He looks mildly worried, less reptilian.

"Yeah. I'm pretty sure I mentioned it," I say.

We walk through to the kitchen.

"Can you eat before this thing?" he asks.

"Yes. And I have to drink at least a litre of water. We don't have long though. What did you bring?"

"Sushi."

"It looks fancy," she says, impressed and coming round to the idea of his unplanned appearance.

"It is. I'm told the chefs are very good."

"It doesn't seem like much for three," I say.

"It looks like plenty," says Lyd, looking at me insipidly.

My ego is a little bit drunk on the fact that Peter seems unable to belittle me for a change. I have to be placated and fed posh sushi. This must be about Gloria.

(Lyd now knows about Sergio running off with Mitsu and that Gloria has been sleeping with someone else but she doesn't know that Peter is that someone.)

"So, why aren't you at work?" I ask him.

Lyd walks over to the cupboards and starts gathering

plates and chopsticks. Me and Peter sit down facing each other, leaving the middle seat for Lyd.

"Oh, you know, business lunch."

"You finance boys don't do a thing in your big offices all day," I say. "I bet you could disappear for a year and they wouldn't notice."

"*Vince*," says Lyd. "If you're trying to say thank you for the lovely food I think you're getting it a bit wrong."

"He's probably right," says Peter, attempting a laugh but failing. "Sometimes I look at what's in front of me and I'm not even sure what I do."

"I'm sure that's just because it's complicated," she says, putting plates down on the table.

"Maybe," he says, sighing.

Lyd opens the boxes of sushi and starts putting the pieces on a big central plate.

"Are you..." Lyd pauses, looking at me sharply before settling back on Peter tenderly, "okay?"

"Of course. You know me," he says, with a complete lack of the piercing charm he is so well known for.

He takes two hosomaki rolls off the middle plate and covers them in soy. Lyd finds a little tub of wasabi at the bottom of the brown paper bag and passes it his way. She serves out the rest of the sushi, puts the empty boxes back in the bag and leaves the bag on the floor by her chair, out of the way, for recycling as soon as she's done eating.

"How's the writing going?" asks Peter, smearing wasabi on the vinegared rice of one of his rolls.

"You should probably avoid the tuna," I say to Lyd. She looks baffled. "Mercury." She rolls her eyes and takes a tuna and avocado futomaki from the centre. I look at Peter. "I've been in a bit of a difficult patch. I think I might be coming out of it now."

"Are you allowed to tell us what it's about yet?" he asks.

"I'm not very good at talking about my work," I say. "I'm better at describing the process."

"Oh well," he says. "Keep trucking and all that."

Lyd's head is moving back and forth between us, mildly suspicious about how polite her brother is being.

"How are things with you?" I ask.

Peter pauses at the question, his chopsticks hovering. He sniffs, looks down at his plate and a desperately lonely smile creeps onto his face.

"I think I might be in love," he says.

"That's great," says Lyd, sympathetic now that she feels that she has the missing link. "Pascale is so perfect."

Peter looks up at her, confused, the momentary wet sheen on his eyes dull again.

"Who?" he asks.

"Pascale," I say, for her.

"Yes… Pascale… No… I'm not in love with Pascale."

I take a large spicy salmon temaki from the centre.

"It must have been a whirlwind romance," I say.

Lyd shows me the whites of her eyes.

"Not really," he replies. "It's been on the cards for a while. It just seemed… impossible. Like it couldn't really be happening. Pascale was just a distraction. I'm done with Pascale."

"So, who's the lucky lady?" I ask.

"Yes. Who is she?"

"I can't… I mean, I'm not ready to talk about her."

"Just the process," I say.

"Yes," he replies, with an amused lilt.

We eat the rest of the sushi. Peter, besides sniffing occasionally, is quiet. I tilt the conversation towards the dating scan. Lyd looks puzzled. I can see that she's already building a deep defence against this woman whose love has dimmed the sparkling elegance of her brother.

I clear the plates once we're done and leave them to chat for a minute while I wash up and put the recycling out. When I come back in from the bins I hear Lyd say:

"Right, I'm going to pop to the loo before I have to drink all this water."

The second she leaves the kitchen Peter stands up and rushes over to me.

"You *have* to talk to her for me, Vince. I *need* to see her."

"Gloria?"

"She won't answer my calls. She's not answering the door. I'm afraid there might be something wrong with her. Something might have *happened*."

His gruff intensity is suddenly back, but fuelled by anxiety rather than the usual egomania. My raised palms are doing nothing to ease him away from me.

"Slow down," I say. "Calm down."

"I'm serious."

"You can't pull me further into this thing. I feel bad enough about lying to Lyd as it is. Have either of you thought about when you're going to tell her?"

"I'm going out of my mind here. I know you don't like me. I know Sergio's your friend. But *please*. I just need you to do this one thing."

"Did you hear me? You need to tell Lyd. You're ruining one of her favourite friendships. You're forcing me into a position where I have to lie to her. Does any of this mean anything to you?"

"I wouldn't ask unless I was desperate."

I'm momentarily astounded by this admission. His honesty coerces me the way his charisma coerces others. I find myself nodding.

"Okay. I'll pop round," I say. "But this is the only time I'm getting involved. I don't want to know about this stuff. You need to keep me out of it."

He puts both of his huge hands on the sides of my head.

"When? *When*?"

"Today, if I get a chance. Tomorrow, maybe. But remember, I'm only doing this so you two can talk about how to tell Lyd. Whether it's over or not, one of you needs to tell her."

"Let me know as soon as you've seen her. *Please*. And let

me know if it's going to be tomorrow. I can't sit around all night not knowing."

"I'll text you later."

He releases my head and hugs me with forceful gratitude.

"Thank you, Vince. I mean it."

He lets go of me and waits around for Lyd, unable to meet my eyes. Purpose fulfilled, ashamed of his display of weakness, he's ready to leave. When Lyd walks back in he quickly perks up and grabs her for a hug.

"Got to dash, sis. Got to go and sit in my office and pretend to do some work."

"Okay," she laughs. "You seem very chipper all of a sudden."

"He's a good man, this one," he says, unclasping one of his arms from her and pointing at me. "You keep hold of him."

He kisses her cheek and sees himself out.

"Bye," she calls.

"Bye," I echo.

Lyd looks at me with disbelief and, as soon as the front door closes, asks:

"What was that about?"

"I have no idea."

"What did you say to him whilst I was gone?"

"I just fed him some line about love. I can't remember."

"I knew you'd grow on him eventually," she says, a deep confirmation forming within her. "You're good with people when they're down."

"Sure," I say. "It was bound to happen sooner or later."

"Still, he was acting weird. I'm a bit worried about him."

"Yes," I agree. "Not himself, was he?"

After drinking a litre of water, Lyd drives us to the clinic. In the waiting room her leg is jigging up and down. She already needs to urinate and, because she doesn't understand why she isn't allowed to, she's feeling aggressive and annoyed about it. Her arms are crossed and her elbows are hunched up. I stare at the other couples in the waiting room and decide that we're the best one, the one I want to be a part of.

We're called through.

The sonographer has the self-satisfied posture of a person who feels like he is doing something good with his life. His smile gives the impression that, because he thinks that he lives in the presence of miracles, he has different priorities and understandings to the rest of us. He is only slightly grounded by the occasions on which he has had to deliver serious or bad news and goes about his work with an air of mild bliss.

I am envying his charmed mind. Lyd is half sitting/half lying on an electronic examination bed staring at him, trying to scratch out his harmless conceit with invisible claws.

"Can you just hitch your top up to your ribs for me?" he says.

She does.

"That's great. You might have to undo your trousers and pull them down but they've got quite a low waist so let's see if we can get a peak without. I'm going to rub some of this gel on your stomach. It'll be quite cold and I'll have gloves on so it might feel a little bit strange, okay? I know you're probably bursting for the toilet, and there's going to be some pressure on your bladder, but try to relax."

Lyd smiles with discomfort, glad that her situation has been acknowledged, and nods.

Once the skin over her womb is covered in lubricant he wheels over a machine that is much more hi-tech than the one that was used at Charlie's ultrasounds. It has a thousand knobs and dials, a touch pad, devices with curly wires hooked onto the side, a big monitor on top and a large vaginal probe sticking up on the right-hand edge.

The sonographer grabs the transducer from the nodule beneath the probe and moves it over Lyd's lubricated stomach. Four grainy images immediately flicker onto the monitor, and dials and bars light up all over the machine's surfaces. He presses a few buttons on the touch screen and twists a few knobs. Lyd's initial unease from the pressure on her bladder quickly dissipates into curiosity, knowing that all the lights and measurements are derived from her body and its systems.

"Nicely placed… It's over seven centimetres and just starting to curl so you must be around fourteen weeks… The heartbeat looks good… No major structural abnormalities visible, but we'll know more about that next time. Have you had any bleeding? Light spotting?"

"No. Nothing like that. Would that be bad?"

"Not necessarily."

My eyes are fixed on the screen but I can't see anything. I don't even have an inkling of what they could be looking at. I have a creeping suspicion that we're not seeing the same thing. My screen is blank. It's empty. There's no life, just a bit of green fuzz.

"Everything looks great," he says.

"It's got a face," says Lyd. "Oh my God. It's got a face."

She squeezes my hand.

"Yes," he confirms.

"Yeah," I agree, but it still seems like a blank womb full of pointless squiggles and dots to me.

I don't want a new baby, I hear myself think, but not in my own inner voice. It's something more direct, more instantaneous, coming from nowhere.

"Can we tell if it's a girl or a boy?" asks Lyd. "Wait. I'm not sure I want to know."

"You're a bit further on than we thought, so we could have a good guess, but think it over. You'll be able to know for sure at your anomaly scan."

The word *anomaly* makes my stomach turn.

"No, actually. I don't think we want to know," she says. "Not yet."

"No," I mumble, in agreement.

I feel light-headed.

The sonographer says something I can't hear, takes the transducer off Lyd's stomach and gives her some tissues to wipe off the gel. I'm still looking at the blank screen wondering why I didn't see it.

After the scan Lyd goes to try out a yoga class for pregnant women that she's found online. Whilst she's out the house I take the opportunity to visit Gloria. It's less than a fifteen-minute walk from ours.

Sergio's vintage mahogany MGB GT V8 is parked in the driveway. Sitting in the passenger seat, Mitsu waits with her arms folded, disgusted with everything. She is dressed like a schoolgirl again but with an additional neo-western shoestring necktie clasped with a silver skull.

I wave, keeping my enthusiasm in check. Her eyes slowly track over towards me, acknowledge nothing and move back to their prior position. I sarcastically give her a false suburban smile and salute. She stares gloomily ahead.

The front door is open so I put a foot inside and crane my head over the threshold. I can hear Spanish words violently slashing through the air from upstairs.

"Hello?"

The two voices continue to bicker.

"*Hello*?"

There is a momentary lapse in sound before the squabble starts up again, getting louder and louder until I can pretty much gauge the full volume of it coming down from the top of the stairs. Sergio is shouting with amused disdain. Gloria is screaming with the emotional volatility of somebody surprised about how hurt she is.

Sergio comes down the stairs with two suitcases. Gloria is throwing shirts and trousers down the stairs after him, along with torrents of verbal abuse. Seeing me, Sergio frowns for a moment before shouting back up the stairs:

"Whore!"

"Pervert!" she shouts back.

A shoe flies down at him. He flinches, trying to move out of the way, but it hits his shoulder.

"Psycho!" he shouts.

He picks up the shoe and throws it back up the stairs at her before turning and walking quickly past me, barging my shoulder and ignoring me. He looks terrible. The last few weeks with Mitsu have aged him. Perhaps he is just sleep deprived from an overactive sex life but I get a deep sense of loss and loneliness from his eyes.

Sergio rushes to his car, throwing his suitcases into the boot. Gloria screams in Spanish again and comes rushing down the stairs with rage so blind that my stomach lifts. She doesn't even notice me as she rushes out the front door holding the shoe that was thrown back and forth between them.

Sergio climbs into the driver's seat and pushes down the lock just in time. Gloria is pulling on the door handle and when one of her fingernails snaps she screams up into the air, cursing his "stupid, precious car", and then starts hammering the heel of the shoe down on the windscreen, where his face is.

She manages three ineffective smashes before something occurs to her. She looks around the garden with fierce alacrity and rushes over to the garden wall as Sergio reverses out of the driveway.

"Jesus," I hear myself mutter as she runs out of the garden with half a brick poised above her head.

Sergio, seeing her coming for him, slams the accelerator down but he's not quite fast enough. The brick crunches against his rear right tail light, which pops and shatters, leaving a trail of red plastic and clear glass as he speeds away.

Gloria immediately starts stamping her way back up the driveway. There is a tiny flicker of recognition as she sees me standing in front of her house.

"Gloria," I begin, in an apologetic tone, "it's about Peter."

She strides past me and into the house.

"Fuck off, Vince," she says, before slamming the door in my face.

I think about knocking on the door but turn to leave instead. Sergio's shoe is still in the middle of the driveway.

TWO

The dawn chorus becomes particularly loud and full during the mornings around the summer solstice. Skylarks, song thrushes, robins and blackbirds chime in first, before the sun has risen. Then sparrows, finches and buntings add their twitters and trills. Warblers and wrens wait for the sunlight but soon catch up. Adults call. Chicks cry. Each kind uses a different frequency and only sings to its own but together the birds fill the sky with a song that is as predestined but chaotic as the pathway a growing tree takes to the sun; all the gaps are filled, not a drop of silence is wasted.

Since the dating scan I can't get it out of my head that our baby doesn't exist but I also vaguely remember having some trouble with screens after Charlie's death; a bus that was heading to *Black Hole*, a shadowy cashpoint where every option was *Death*. I don't feel like I've lost my grip on reality to that extent but I have to be careful this doesn't go too far. A few days ago I woke in the middle of the night and said:

"The photo. There must be a photo."

Lyd stirred.

"Where's the photo?" I asked her. "The photo of the baby. The sonogram."

"Go… sleep," she mumbled.

"Did we get a photo, a picture, at the dating scan?"

"No… forgot."

She rolled away from me.

For a brief moment, I thought I'd saved myself.

It's the weekend now and I don't want it to be. The weekend means I have to face Lyd and I'm so anxious at the moment that I'm afraid I won't be able to hide it for the full two days. I managed to get through the weekday evenings by being quiet and staying out of her way.

She's already left the bedroom when I wake up. I get up and look out the window. The sky is low and dull. There have been showers and bursts of sunshine all week; mild drizzle, warm sunny patches, rainbows, cold hard rain, fast clouds breaking apart. Today the sky has no shifting characteristics, just a low, paper-white ceiling that will last all day.

I've still not heard anything from Angela about the chapters I sent to her so I'm currently trying to blame her for a lot of my feelings of anxiety (unsuccessfully). I quickly check my email before I go downstairs: still nothing.

In the kitchen, Lyd is holding a cup and staring out into the back garden with a mildly confounded look on her face.

"What's up?" I ask.

"Huh?"

"You look confused?"

"No," she says. "Not really. The birds woke me up at four thirty this morning, they were ridiculously loud, and it's bright so early at the moment, I couldn't get back to sleep, we really need better curtains by the way, but, have you noticed, they're not singing at all now? The birds."

I listen. It's true. There's no birdsong in the air. I shrug, open the sliding door, wait a few seconds and whistle. Blackie doesn't appear.

"I wonder why they've abandoned us," she says.

"Maybe a sultana factory exploded and they all went to visit."

Lyd smiles.

"You've got *me* fixated on the bloody birds now," she says, dismissing her curiosity.

I step out onto the patio. There's a little bit of birdsong

but it's sparrows and robins and other small birds. The loud and distinctive blackbird solos are the main thing missing. I walk out into the middle of the lawn and look up and around. Turning back towards the house a dark shape catches my eye. I approach it for a closer look.

A female blackbird lies on her back, her wings inaccurately flailed out, head turned to the side, motionless, dead. Her stomach has been ripped open and an inch and a half of her pink-and-red guts are hanging out.

My throat is closing. I'm getting dizzy. Breathing is difficult. I close my eyes and take a moment to inhale and exhale slowly. It's just a dead bird but I feel overwhelmed by its death. I have to get away from it. I go back into the kitchen.

"What's wrong?" asks Lyd, as I walk towards her.

I fall on my knees in front of her and wrap my arms around her pelvis, pulling her melon-sized womb towards my head.

"Nothing," I say.

"Vince? What's going on? What are you doing?"

As my disorientation passes I realise that this is not normal behaviour. Lyd is trying to wriggle away from me. I let go, stand up and try to make light of it.

"Nothing. Really. I'm fine. I just wanted to listen to the baby for a minute… Sorry. I didn't mean to freak you out."

"You wanted to listen to the baby?"

"I had an uncontrollable urge."

"Right."

"I think I solved the mystery, anyway."

"Mystery?"

"Next door's cat's killed a blackbird in our garden. Must have scared all the others off. Her guts are hanging out."

"Gross," says Lyd, putting a hand on her stomach.

"I don't feel like I can just throw her in the bin. It's not like finding a dead mouse."

"No?"

"I think I might bury her in the garden. If that's okay?"

"Put some Marigolds on. They're full of parasites."

"Okay."

My hands are trembling as I dig near the fence with a trowel. I can feel Lyd's glare burning my back. I'm trying not to make a big show of it but I am trying to appease the blackbirds. This is a test, or a sign, part of their system of guidance, but it also feels threatening, dark, like they want me to live in fear. By burying her I'm showing that I respect their lives and hold their species in high regard, that I will contemplate the meaning of this sacrifice.

The grave is around seven inches deep when I'm done. I put the bird in and scatter mud over her. When she's covered I feel the need to enact some form of ritual but I don't know what to do. I think of priests reciting prayers and making the sign of the cross but these things don't apply to me so I simply bow my head to offer a moment of quiet reverence.

When I get back inside Lyd kisses me on the cheek. There is a dismissive sympathy in the way her lips make contact with my skin that makes me feel awkward and judged.

"Chuck them out," she says, pointing with her eyes down at the yellow rubber gloves.

I smile and put them in the bin. She goes through to the living room. I follow her in. She's picking up a thesis that's been sitting half-read on the coffee table for weeks.

"Do we have anything planned for today?" I ask.

She looks up from her pages and around the room. Something occurs to her.

"What?" I ask.

"Are there more cushions than there used to be?"

"What do you mean?"

"More cushions."

"No," I say.

"There never used to be this many cushions."

"There's been this many for ages."

"Where did they all come from?"

I sigh.

"There were two in Charlie's room."

"In Charlie's room?" she asks.

"In the moon."

"You destroyed the moon?"

Lyd grabs one of the cushions and holds it to her stomach. I sigh again.

"What was I supposed to do with it?"

"I thought you boxed everything up? What else did you throw away?"

"Nothing. I just had to throw that thing away. I couldn't keep it."

"How have I not noticed all these cushions?"

"I don't know."

"If we could have only kept one thing I'd have said keep the moon."

"Of course you would."

"I *would*. He loved that thing."

"Some things are too painful to keep."

"And some things are too painful to throw away."

"Can we not do this, please? It's done. There's nothing I can do about it."

"Fine."

She shuffles her legs beneath her, still gripping the cushion firmly. She puts the thesis down.

"Let's go and buy a crib," she says.

"What? Really?"

"My headaches and soreness are beginning to level off. And I'll be the size of a planet before long. I'm in the sweet spot for getting things done. Besides, we're not going to have a good time today. We may as well tick a box."

"Sounds fun."

Lyd drives us to a place that's a bit like IKEA. It stands alone off a busy dual carriageway, has the same drawn-out shopping procedure and the same homogenised but stylish produce, but it's more expensive. I think IKEA does "style on a budget" well, so you may as well get the cheap stuff, but Lyd likes to spend a little bit more and feel like she has quality products. She says that materials matter and I agree, but I don't think they use better materials. Still, that's where we go. Since crashing the car during my breakdown, she's the one who drives.

In the car I'm trying to look at Lyd and think about her beauty and the happiness of our future life together, the simple but stylish furniture we'll be surrounded by, but she's grimacing.

"What's wrong?" I ask.

"I can hear the blood in my veins," she says, flicking a wrist around as though shooing the sensation away.

"*Hear* it?"

She nods, clutching the steering wheel with disgust.

"I wonder if you're hearing through the baby's ears?"

"I doubt it."

"Amazing."

"Not really. It's making me feel sick. I don't want to talk about it."

"Okay."

The gigantic car park is full. We have to drive around aimlessly waiting for someone to pull out. For a couple of minutes we slowly follow a man carrying a huge box of flat-packed wood until he gets so edgy that he stops to let us past. We stop too, thinking he's at his car, and the three of us end up looking at each other in a confused triangle. Eventually, somebody pulls out twenty metres ahead of him so Lyd floors the accelerator, which makes him flinch and lose his grip on his giant box.

Walking towards the ugly, grey warehouse with its glassy, corporate entranceway a low flying blackbird swoops above my head releasing a flurry of loud tweets:

– *chuck-chicka-chink choo-chucka-chucka pook-pook-pook* –

(*Watch out. The chaos is coming.*)

My stomach turns and the speed and proximity of its flight makes me duck slightly.

"What's wrong?" asks Lyd.

"Did you see that?"

"See what?"

"You must have heard it."

"What?"

I'm unsure if she's daring me to draw attention to *yet another* blackbird or if she didn't see or hear it at all. I look up at the empty white sky.

"Never mind," I say.

I catch a glint of disgust in Lyd's expression and note that I've seen her look at me like that a few times in the last couple of weeks.

We walk towards the entranceway with a metre between our shoulders.

"You know, we still have a crib," I say, as the automatic doors slide open. "In the attic."

This comes out at the worst possible moment. It's my version of a nervous tick. I have a knack for finding the exact wrong thing to say at the exact wrong moment. Lyd is aware of this facet so she just glances at me sullenly. Thankfully, she's forgotten that I stopped doing this when I started taking lithium.

"I want everything new," she says. "I don't care what we've already got."

"That's going to be expensive."

"It's my money."

"I'm aware of that."

As we turn the first corner we find ourselves standing at the foot of a corridor of fake living rooms full with a near-impenetrable amount of people. In this shop you can't just find the thing you need and buy it. You have to walk through a whole labyrinth of jumbled produce, note down everything that you want and wait to see if they have it in stock when you get to the end.

Lyd glances at me, subtly amused, knowing that this is many of my least favourite things crammed into one experience:

a packed crowd, a cynically inefficient system, overpriced products, pretentious parents, identikit individualism, squealing children... My teeth are firmly clenched.

Lyd is much more well adjusted than me and sees this place as a gift to consumers with good taste. To her it's a chance for people of average wealth to afford the luxury of excellent design without the hackneyed feeling that it is too cheap and commonplace.

"Let's just get this over with," I say.

"Lead the way."

I push through the centre of the crowd in silence, evading cellulite hips and bony shoulders, moving forward at four times the normal customer rate. We get to the children's bedrooms before the baby rooms. I've stopped because I've seen Charlie's wardrobe. Lyd notices what I'm looking at.

"I don't mind so much about that sort of thing," she says. "Maybe we could re-use the wardrobe? He didn't spend any time in it. Touching it. You know?"

"No."

"No?"

"We should get all new, like you said."

"But..."

"The wardrobe's got his stickers all over it."

(And I smashed it to smithereens.)

"I suppose you're right. Do you think we'll need a wardrobe straight away? When did we get one for Charlie?"

I shrug and Lyd carries on talking about other things we might need but I'm not listening properly. I'm looking around for the red 1960s robot as if, by some trick of fate, it will be decorating one of these fake children's bedrooms and I'll be able to grab it and use it to smash the whole store to pieces.

"So?"

"What?" I ask.

"What planet are you on today?"

"We probably won't need a new chest of drawers," I say, clutching at an echoed memory of her speaking.

"I thought you just said you didn't want us to reuse anything."

"There's no stickers on the drawers. I left them in the room. We don't need more drawers. They won't fit up the hatch into the attic. There's no point throwing drawers away and getting the same replacement drawers."

"What's wrong with you?"

"What are you talking about?"

"You're clenching your fists. Your knuckles are white."

"I just hate it in here."

"Come on. I can see a crib down there."

We take down the product number, buy the overpriced crib and get out of there. It's a simple white thing. Yet, for all its simplicity, back home, it takes me about four and a half hours to construct. The whole time I'm thinking that I must be a terrible writer because Angela still hasn't been in touch. I know my expectations are usually too high when I give people things to read but she was so positive about my first two novels. The way she responds to my work has changed my life. Now she doesn't even have a response.

The crib is done but the baby room still looks undefined. It's devoid of character, completely white, just the bare essentials. It isn't Charlie's room anymore though. Charlie has been whitewashed out of the space. For some reason, this notion reminds me of the blank screens at the dating scan. There's nothing in Lyd's womb. There's no baby. Why do I keep thinking this?

I go to my office and check my email. Still nothing. Nothing from anyone. I click on my junk folder, select all and delete them. Immediately, that weird piece of junk email returns:

From: *CHARLIE*

Subject: (276) Re: contact me please…

I decide that it's finally time to open it and click on the title.

Dear Sir/Madam

I am Charlie a Banker working in bank in London Until now I am account officer to most government accounts and I have since discovered that most of the account are dormant account with a lot of money in on further investigation I found out that one particular account belong to the former minister MR Dennis McShane, who ruled Rotherham from 1994-2012 and this particular account has deposit of £146,000 with no next of kin.

My proposal is that since I am the account officer and the money on the account is dormant and there is no next of kin obviously the account owner the former president of Rotherham has died, that you should provide an account for the money to be transferred.

The money is floating in the bank right now and I want to transfer to your account for our mutual benefit. Please if this is okay by you I will advice that you contact me through my direct email address.

Your reply will be appreciated,
Thank you.
CHARLIE

I'm glad that I've finally read it. Having deleted it so many times, it was beginning to seem like an unstoppable force in my life. Its persistence had made me think that it really might be from Charlie, because it was behaving like my memory of him behaves. I'm amused by how relieved I am about the fact that it's just the usual sort of scam but then I feel sad about Charlie, sad that I've been whitewashing his memory out of our lives. Then it occurs to me why I saw a blank screen at the ultrasound. I click reply and start writing.

Dear Charlie,

I hope you know that you are still a very real part of my life. The pain of losing you was so intense that I had a breakdown. When I started putting myself back together again there was a little part of you in every single piece. You became part of me, so I could never lose you.

As you know, me and your mum are going to have another baby. I don't want you to be jealous about this. Nobody will ever replace you. I know you probably want me to forget about the new baby but I have to be its father and try to love it. I want us all to stay together. Please try to understand. Try to let me be happy.

Love from,
Daddy

I click send. A couple of seconds later a new message appears in my junk folder.

From: *CHARLIE*
 Subject: (1) Re: direct contact…

I click the cross in the top right corner and close the Internet window. That's enough communicating with my dead son for one day.

After a near silent dinner, I spend the rest of the evening reading through my first six chapters again; deleting an adverb here, changing a comma there, wondering what it is that links these stories together. I don't dare write for fear of casting my net too wide, creating blind alleys and unanswerable questions. I need the idea to talk to me before I move forward but the project has become silent and inert.

Lyd is asleep when I get into bed. She looks peaceful.

Sometimes I forget how much grief there is inside her whilst she's awake. This is how her face used to be, especially in the mornings, before all the mathematics and physics started creeping back into her head.

I'm trying to stay still so I don't wake her but I can tell that it's going to be another sleep deprived night. I've always been unable to wind down at the end of the day. It seemed like I spent half of my childhood lying awake in bed. This is something that lithium helped me to forget. Its chemical fuzz allowed me to slip into sleep in minutes.

Thirty or forty minutes later I'm trying to control my breathing, easing my brain into unconsciousness, when I hear the pitter-patter of tiny feet run across the ceiling. My body tenses up and my heart starts beating fast. Lyd, sleeping next to me, rolls over, momentarily disturbed, and makes a quiet moaning sound.

I get out of bed and walk down the dark hallway. As I get to the baby's room I stop and put my ear to the door. It's silent in there. I turn the doorknob and walk in. The curtains are open so it's marginally lighter than the hallway. Everything is still. The room is white, soulless. The empty crib sits in the corner.

Little feet run along the ceiling again, directly over my head.

"Charlie?" I whisper.

I pull the string that unlocks the attic door and lower the pull-down ladder, slowly to make doubly sure I don't wake Lyd. The thin metal crossbeams hurt my feet as I ease my weight onto each step. My heart is racing. My throat is dry.

My head emerges above the floor of the attic.

"Charlie?" I whisper again.

There's a faint giggle, over in the corner.

"Charlie?"

I climb up into the attic and after two steps nearly trip over a box of Christmas decorations. I stop still, listening for Lyd. I don't think I've disturbed her.

Moving the box aside, I remember tinsel in Lyd's hair and Charlie banging his spoon about in his high chair, cranberry sauce all over his face. A new toy fire engine that he wouldn't eat without is knocked to the floor. He doesn't cry, he giggles. I hear this same giggle to the side of me.

I keep a torch by the edge of the hatch so I grab it and turn it on. I shine it to the right side of the attic, where the giggle came from. The yellow spot of illumination passes over Charlie's empty high chair.

There's a lot of his stuff up here now; his crib, boxes full of bottles and bibs. Then there's all the things from his room. Everything he ever had.

A round shadow swings across the back wall and disappears behind the boxes full of Charlie's toys.

I close my eyes for a couple of seconds. I try to tell myself that these sounds and shadowy movements are not real, they are symptoms, but either way I know I have to face them. A tear slips down my right cheek, my hands are shaking. What if I see his face?

I approach the pile of boxes where the round shadow vanished. A new noise is coming from behind the boxes now, one my brain can't decipher. My ears are struggling to hear Charlie but the dots don't connect. The sound is distorted, lost between two places, like a dream language scrambling into nonsense as I wake.

I move towards this fuzzy sound and peer behind the boxes. The noise becomes louder, more high-pitched. I shine the torch into the corner and see something tiny moving down on the floor. My eyes won't inform me as to what it is. To get a closer look, because of the slope of the roof, I have to get down on all fours.

As I lower myself, my knee crunches on a horrible cone-shaped object full of painful little nubs. I almost cry out but breathe through the sides of my teeth instead. I shine the torch towards the object and see the red 1960s robot. I stand it up by the sidewall and look back into the corner.

After this small bout of pain everything is clear and focused. There are three little fledglings chirping in a small round nest. A quick look around reveals that there's a crack in one of the nearby roof tiles through which the mother must have been coming and going.

"Vince?"

I crawl backwards, sliding the nest along with me, then stand up and see the silhouette of Lyd's head popping up from the hatch.

"It's okay, honey," I say. "Go back to bed."

"What are you doing?"

"It's just a nest of chicks. I heard them chirping. That dead bird today must have been their mother."

"Chicks?"

"Yes."

"Are they okay?"

"They're distressed. I'm going to take them outside, put them in the evergreen next to the other nest."

"Now?"

"Yes. They'll die up here on their own."

"You scared me."

"I'm sorry, honey," I say, carefully lifting the nest.

"I thought it was Charlie."

"What?" I ask, quickly turning my head towards the hatch.

"I hope they're not starving."

"They'll be fine," I say. "Go on."

"Do you want me to leave the light on down here?"

"No, my eyes have adjusted."

"Okay. Night."

"Night, love."

I carry the nest over to the hatch and carefully sit down with my heels on the ladder. I turn off the torch, leaving it in its usual place, and descend the rungs slowly, putting my weight onto my pelvis, sitting on each crossbeam to stop my heels from slipping out from under me.

120

By the time I make it to the ground the three chicks are frantic, squealing for food, scared. I hold them towards the window to see them better. They have no feathers and there are still shards of egg around them. Their skin is purply-pink and their eyes big and blind.

As I walk them through the hall, Lyd calls:

"I can hear them."

"Do you want to see?" I ask.

"No. I think it might upset me."

"Okay. I'll be up in a bit."

I carry the nest downstairs and through to the kitchen. I have to put them down on the counter whilst I open the sliding door. Brisk air rushes in. I'm still barefoot and in my boxer shorts but I can't be bothered going to get dressed. It will only take a minute. I'm worried about exposing the featherless chicks to it but I decide that most chicks are outside and that it might be warmer in the middle of a bush. This is their only chance.

Out in the back garden, their chirping is dampened. They seem quieter and smaller heard alongside the sounds of the wind and the moving leaves and branches. Or perhaps, beneath the sky, they have sensed danger and actively become more discreet; a warning from their genetic memory.

I walk over to the spot where Blackie and his partner live. At the foot of the evergreen I hold the nest forward and try to move one of the bigger branches aside with the outside of my wrist. As I do this I hear an aggressive:

– *SEEEEEEEE!* –

An extremely irate female blackbird rushes out of the bush and flies at my face. I fall backwards and drop the nest. I have no time to regroup and check the chicks because the bird, Blackie's partner, is following through with her attack.

I feel a sharp peck on the top of my head.

– *SEEEEEEEE!* –

A tiny talon scratches my cheek.

The fluttering of wings seems to be everywhere. I turn my back to her and scramble away from the bush. There's another peck on the back of my neck, one on my shoulder and then one at the back of my ankle. After that she's gone, back to her nest and chicks.

I sit on the edge of the patio to collect myself for a moment. The surface is cold and quickly brings me back to my senses. I cautiously step sideways, moving back towards the bush with my head lowered and my elbow up. The nest is upside down on the lawn.

As I get closer I see one of the chicks about thirty centimetres from the nest. It's still and quiet and has died at some point in the commotion; perhaps from the fall, maybe I scrambled over it.

I lurk down even lower, sending my knees out sideways, and tip up the edge of the nest. Beneath, the two remaining fledglings immediately raise their beaks into the air and begin chirping. I delicately place them back into the slightly dishevelled nest. One of them tries to feed from my finger as I lift it. It occurs to me that I might be issuing these chicks a death sentence (without their mother to keep them warm) but I don't know what else to do. I go to the other end of the garden and embed them as deep into the evergreen as I can.

I pick the dead chick up off the lawn, careful not to split its thin skin open, and carry it to its mother's grave. It's still warm. I scoop out a couple of handfuls of dirt and then bury it. I tell myself that this does not have to be a sign. My life and the blackbirds' lives are not cosmically engaged. It could mean anything. If it was a test it could have been to see if I would feel a sense of duty, a need to nurture, a desire to protect. I'm making a vested effort not to think the worst.

Wincing at the chirps of the chicks I have left alone in the bush, I head back inside, wash my hands, check to see if

Blackie's partner broke my skin (she didn't) and climb back into bed. Lyd is asleep and keeps her back to me. I stare up at the ceiling, wondering if I'll ever hear those pitter-pattering feet again.

THREE

In an old myth, a prankster promises two lovers that one day they will find a pot of gold at the foot of a rainbow, just so long as they hold on to each other. Wandering through the greenest lands, they rush towards each rainbow they find with their arms and shoulders entwined, the promise finally coming true, but as they near the point where the colours touch the ground the pair always find their arms untangling and their hands pulling apart. They are never quite heading in the same direction and, at the vital moment, they always separate, each blaming the other for running the wrong way. All their lives they never once imagine that they are seeing two separate rainbows. It's right there in front of them, right in the centre of their world.

After signing in at reception and getting a visitor's card, I swipe through the barriers and walk into the lobby. It's a vast space. The back wall is a fifty-foot black marble monolith. The six lifts and two stairway entrances are framed with brass. The sidewalls are white-polished oak. The floor is covered with giant black rectangular tiles with embedded flakes of silver and crystal. I can't remember which side I'm supposed to get the lift on.

Two black marble doors open in the centre of the shiny back wall; an executive elevator I didn't know was there. Curious, I look over to see who's coming out and immediately fill with disgust. It's Ajwan White; a writer whose work I hate.

He's one of these accidental zeitgeist novelists who continually trades off the success of his first book. His work is gimmicky and full of cheap tricks but a passing fashion for "spiritual postmodernism" meant that he was given a big marketing budget. All his main characters are narcissistic idiots who have big epiphanies and then change for the better.

I'm trying to look away, to choose between right or left, but something seems to be wrong with him. He moves his spine diagonally backwards. He ducks down and runs forward. He scratches manically at his ear with both hands. He turns one hundred and eighty degrees, ducks lower, then turns one hundred and eighty degrees again. Just as he looks like he's going to calm down, his spine jolts and he flings his right arm out in a big arc.

Watching him, I feel a little bit light-headed. The black marble swells and distorts. I close my eyes for a couple of seconds. When I open them he is looking around, panicking again, and he starts running back towards the lift. The black marble doors are sliding closed, he's not fast enough, and he ends up pushed against them. He quickly turns and looks in the air around him. His nerves begin to settle. He walks away from the shiny black wall grinning and shaking his head.

I'm standing in the centre of the lobby and still haven't chosen left or right. Despite the fact that I'm clearly just watching him I'm also eager to imply that I'm not interested in the fact that he's walking towards me.

"Did you see that?" he asks, smug, amazed by something pitiful, probably about to "change" for the better.

I look over my shoulder to check for other people. He's talking to me. The bastard is talking to me.

"What?" I ask, annoyed with myself for engaging.

He laughs, leans down, puts his hands on his knees and breaths deeply for a second. He's bathing in my attention. Pathetic.

"Phew! There was a wasp waiting for me when the lift doors opened. It came right at me."

"A wasp?"

"I *know*."

"I thought you'd lost it."

"I nearly did… I'd love to know if they get a kick out of doing that to people."

"I doubt it."

He looks around and decides he can finally be fully calm.

"Sorry, but you're Vincent Watergate, right?"

"Vince," I say, he doesn't seem to be offering his hand so I'm not either. "And you're Ajwan White?"

"Adge… I heard we were at the same place. Come for your monthly bollocking?"

"Something like that."

"I don't want to keep you. But after the wasp I felt like the ice was already broken… I just wanted to say that I thought *All the Leaves Have Fallen* was… well… you wrote a beautiful book. Really underrated… I can't believe it didn't take off."

"Thanks."

"The relationships, the emotional spectrum, so understated, but so complex. We don't know who to love or who to forgive. Everybody's so… human."

"Thanks."

"Really. I never do this."

"I appreciate it."

"You should be the one doing all the interviews and signings."

"I wouldn't want to," I say. "I read *I Is No More Than the Man Who Says I*."

"A mouthful, isn't it?" He laughs. "God knows how it sold so well."

"Yes. I imagine you sold more than Barthes ever did."

"Thank you," he says, accidentally accepting a compliment that he hasn't been given. "And it's nice that you got the reference. Not many people did. Like I said, a miracle it took off the way it did."

"Advertising," I say. "I suppose corporate investment creates a sense of value."

He finally senses that I'm not a fan. He's not an acute observer.

"Well," he says, amused by my disdain, "I just wanted you to know, you know, how much I enjoy your writing."

He waves awkwardly and walks away shaking his head. At the barriers he pulls out his wallet and holds it over the scanner. It detects the magnetic strip of his entry card inside. The guard nods and smiles at him as he walks out the front door. He doesn't hand in a visitor's card. They must have given him his own card. He can come and go as he pleases.

I take a lift on the left and get lost in a labyrinth of identical corridors, small offices and kooky bureaucrats. After a few horrible minutes I knock on a door and get directions from a woman who looks like I asked if she had a spare kidney.

My agent, Angela "not the dead novelist" Carter, has frizzy brownish-blonde hair cut like an old lady (even though she's not even sixty) and huge glasses that have been in and out of fashion twice since she bought them. Unlike every literary critic in the country, she loved my first two novels.

"Vince. Good to see you."

She says this like a grandmother who once had high hopes for her now disappointing grandson.

"You don't represent Ajwan White, do you?"

"I wish. Ha! No. He's a top-floor author."

"He's a hack."

"Of course he is. Sit down. Sit down... Do you want a drink?"

"I brought you some more pages."

I try to hand her my fourth, fifth and sixth chapters but she puts out her hand in a halting motion, forms a mock-repulsed pout and shakes her head.

"That's not why you're here."

"I'm writing some really good stuff."

"I don't doubt it."

127

She pulls out two crystal glasses and a decent bottle of Glenfiddich from her bottom drawer, pours over an inch into both and offers me the fuller one. I take it.

"It's a little bit disjointed but that's the point. At least, it is at this stage."

"It's great that you're writing again."

"I know it might take readers a little bit of getting into, but I'm pretty sure the pay-off will be worth it in the end."

"Vince, stop. They're turning the screw. Tightening belts. We've got to get rid of our three lowest earners and replace them with one new writer who we're willing to take a risk on. A risk. Ha! That's one way of putting it."

"Shit. Am I one of them? One of the lowest three?"

"You're *the* lowest, darling. I'm sorry. But we've never made a penny out of you. It's like they constantly tell me when I go upstairs: we're not a charity."

"But this is the one. I can feel it. I just need to, wait, do you think Ajwan White is one of his agent's bottom three?"

"I very much doubt it. Why? What's all this Ajwan White talk? Is this book more like what he does?"

"No. *No*. Jesus."

"Too bad."

"It's going to sell. I promise you."

"It's out of my hands."

"So what happens? Do I take my deal somewhere else?"

She sighs.

"That's the other thing I need to tell you. There is no deal."

"What do you mean?"

"I was waiting for the right time. I thought I might be able to sell the rights on to somebody else."

"I don't understand."

"You missed three deadlines, lovey. I know it's been a tough couple of years, and writing's no science, but they can't sit on their hands these days. You signed a contract. Maybe if we were further along… What's it going to be called?"

She picks up a notepad and pen.

"I'm not sure yet. But, wait. I still don't understand. There's no book deal?"

"No."

"So I can't send it to them directly?"

"There is no them. The ship has sailed, come back and sailed again. You'll have to send it to agents, like you did with the first one."

"I got fifty-four rejections before you took it on."

"So you're well-practiced."

"Are you joking? Is this a joke?"

"You can send it to me. When you're done. I'll put it to the top of the slush pile."

"The slush pile?"

"Don't make this harder than it has to be," she says. "Drink your drink."

I take a sip.

"Please. You can't drop me. Lyd's parents already think I'm a failure. This is the only thing I have going for me."

"Right now, the top of the slush pile is the best you can hope for."

"So… I'm fired?"

"Ha! Sorry. Did you ever read your contract? Writers are never really hired, darling. They get picked up."

"And dropped."

"Unfortunately. But it's a business, Vince. And business isn't booming. It used to look good, having a certain spread of talent on the books, but they can't afford to carry people anymore. The culture is changing."

"That's it then?"

"There'll be some paperwork in the post."

"Paperwork?"

"Options. From the publisher. For repaying your advance."

"*Repaying*? I've got a baby on the way. I don't have any income."

"A baby? Congratulations," she says. She means it. "That's wonderful news. But really, doll, how are you surviving? Most of my writers have a second job. Even the successful ones. There's all these creative writing courses popping up. Have you thought about teaching?"

"This can't be happening."

"I'm sorry. I really am. You know I always loved your prose. Do you want another drink?"

"What? No. Thanks."

I get up from my seat.

"Let's not end on a bad note," she says.

"No, of course."

But I'm not with her anymore. I'm retreating, spurned and wounded. I need air. I'm halfway out the door and I don't hear the last thing she says. I'm in the lift swaying and sinking. I'm swiping and swiping but the stupid barrier gate isn't opening.

Rushing out, I get called back by the receptionist. I can't face looking into the eyes of another human being so I pretend I haven't heard her. This only makes the security guard by the door move into the middle of the entrance way. Caught out, I turn back towards the desk. The woman is friendly but I can't communicate. I can barely focus on the portion of the page she wants me to sign after I've given her my visitor's card. She mentions that I should write in the time but this is a step too far. I push the clipboard and her generic pen back at her and walk out past the security guard with my eyes fixed on the ground.

The London streets are full of bright sunlight and car fumes. July is just beginning to get hot. Everybody is dressed for different weather. The busyness of the general street environment is too much for me. I can hear blackbirds singing but I can't see them. Their whistles are mixing with the traffic and people, creating a wall of random, jittery sound. When I put my hands over my ears the birdsong seems louder.

Welcome to the chaos, it says. *Feel free to break down and scream at the sky.*

I rush to the nearest Underground. When I'm on my own I usually prefer the bus but I just want to disappear and reappear where I need to be, get away from this barrage of noise. On the Tube I keep my hands over my ears and rock back and forth in time with the vibrations and whirring and clucking sounds, trying to ignore the jolts and bangs.

When I get back to the house I slam the door on the twittering skies. I hear wittering in the kitchen, faint chirruping behind me. I walk through the hallway to the kitchen. Fee and Dom are sitting at the table with Lyd. They look concerned to the point of tense and Lyd is on the verge of anger.

"What's going on?" I ask. "Why aren't you at work?"

I have not been warned about this visit. I was expecting an empty house. I wanted to lie face down on the bed and shout into a pillow, scrawl neurotic rants about literary agencies and birdsong in my notebook. This is the opposite of what I wanted.

"Lydia needs to talk to you," says Fee.

Lyd whips a warning glance at her mother. I'm struggling to repress thoughts of madness and failure. I take a deep breath and wipe the sweat from my forehead with the back of my hand.

"Lyd?"

She's unsure how to proceed. There is a long pause whilst she tries to phrase things correctly.

"We think you might need some help," says Fee, butting in.

"*Help*? Help with what?" I ask.

"Mum, can you not?" says Lyd.

"We're worried that you're becoming unstable again," says Fee.

"We? Who's we?"

"Myself and Dom," she replies. "And Lydia."

"We're not attacking you," says Dom.

I raise my hand to him.

"Just say what you came to say."

I force myself to take a seat with them at the table. They have had tea and biscuits and a calm, resolved talk in the build-up to this. By comparison, I got denounced by the one thing that set me apart from being a complete failure. I can't even try to project the visage of a calm, centred human being. My legs are jigging and my eyes are wild. I'm holding onto the edge of the table like it's the edge of the Earth.

"Look at yourself," says Fee. "You can barely even sit at a table."

I look at Lyd. She turns away. Dom coughs.

"We just think you maybe need to start seeing someone," he says. "Nothing too serious."

"Lyd, could you please tell me what the hell is going on here?"

"Vince, *stop*," she says, finally looking me in the eyes. "I know… *we* know that you're not taking your medication."

"What?"

"I've known for months."

I glance at Fee and Dom. I hate to admit this breach of trust in front of them.

"Was it Jamal?" I ask. "Did Jamal tell you?"

"Jamal knew?"

"No. I mean… I just thought he might…"

"You can tell Jamal but you can't tell me?"

"No. It's not like that."

"And he knows exactly what happened to you. I'm going to kill that little stoner the next time I see him."

I glance at her parents. They are both fidgeting twitchily after hearing the word "stoner".

"I'm sorry," I say. "Really. But I don't need it. I never did. I lost my grip when Charlie died. That's all. It makes me too fuzzy. I walk into a room and I don't know what I've gone in for. How am I supposed to write when I feel like that?"

"God forbid you should be unable to write," says Lyd.

"We're worried that the news of this baby has set you off again," says Fee.

"Brought up old feelings," says Dom.

"I really can't do this in front of your parents."

"No," she agrees, "I know."

Lyd stands up, glares at her mother and leaves the table. Fee lifts her head diagonally with forced pride to show that she stands by her behaviour. Lyd walks out of the kitchen. I follow her. She turns to me in the hallway.

"This isn't coming from you," I say, quietly. "Do *you* think I should be seeing someone?"

"You should at least see your doctor. You can't just stop taking lithium like that. The rest is up to you."

"I swear, I don't need it."

"I'm still paying a credit card bill that says otherwise."

"Every pill I swallowed was for you."

"And you stop when I get pregnant?" she snaps, folding her arms.

"I just wanted to be me again. For us. For the baby."

"I lost you when I needed you most. I'm not going through that again. I can't risk it. Not with a baby in the house."

"Okay. So we need to talk about it. I know we're not very good at that but we get there in the end. Why did you have to get your parents involved?"

She looks back towards the kitchen and sighs.

"I didn't mean to. I planned to talk to you before they arrived. I meant to do it last night but I lost my nerve. I'm so used to you being free, I forgot about your meeting this morning… I'm going to stay with them for a while."

"You're *leaving*? You can't leave. What about work?"

"There's plenty I can do with an Internet connection. And I'm in Geneva for a fortnight after next week anyway."

"Can you fly?" I ask. "Is it safe?"

"I think so."

"But… What about us?"

"I have no idea what's going on with us. I just know I have to leave."

"When did you decide all this?"

Lyd leans back against the wall and looks up at the ceiling.

"It's too tense for me here. We're in completely different worlds. Things haven't been right since we found out I was pregnant."

"No. But I thought we were working on that. I didn't expect you to run back to your parents."

"I'm not running back to my parents," she says, aggressively. "I've made a decision that I need some distance. The stress here isn't good for me. This is the best way around it."

"You're leaving me, aren't you? They're going to talk you into leaving me."

"Forget about my parents, Vince. It doesn't matter what they want. I'm sorry you had to walk in to that but this has nothing to do with them."

"I stopped taking it for you. I swear."

Lyd shakes her head with disbelief.

"This is broken," she says. "What we have. Here. Surely you can see that? You can't talk to me. I can't talk to you. If we can't be honest about what we're going through then we need to go through it alone."

"Please. Don't do this. Don't leave me."

"Not that you've noticed, but this isn't about you. I've got my own stuff to deal with."

She breaks eye contact, no longer receptive to anything I might say. I know this obstinate look from experience. There's nothing I can do. I try anyway.

"Whatever it is," I say, "you can tell me. I know I've been too self-involved lately but you can always talk to me. I'd never judge you." Her look hardens. My desperation increases. "Can you at least tell me when you're coming back? Are you ever coming back?"

She doesn't respond.

FOUR

Polaris (the North Star) always points true north. This casts the illusion that all the other stars in the sky pivot around it but its actual role in the celestial body is not central and only seems this way due to its relative position to Earth. With its heightened gleam and consistent position, Polaris almost certainly instigated the earliest discoveries of astronomy but it no doubt also helped to elongate the belief that humanity was at the centre of an orchestrated cosmological plan. After all, it is much more probable that the night sky's point of true north would be black, not the brightest star in the sky.

I have a new routine. I wake up at 5am, make myself coffee and toast, feed Blackie and his children and then write and edit in my dressing gown for as long as I can manage. For the first three hours or so my nerves are settled and assured. I invent things, solve problems, make progress, whittle away at words. I don't seem to worry about the value of what I'm doing, or whether all the different stories are ever going to join together. At 5am I can work without doubts.

It's the remaining fifteen hours of my day that I find more difficult. Around 8am my legs begin agitating. The hours ahead seem lonely and vacant. My stomach starts turning. My jaw clenches until my temples ache. I can't imagine the world inside the words I'm working on. The emptiness becomes bigger and wider and harder to ignore until I lose focus completely and I have to face it.

Today, delaying this inevitable confrontation with the big nothing, I visit pregnancy websites and read about the different aspects of the second trimester. Our baby should be beginning to wriggle. It is around six inches long (having doubled in size during the last two weeks). Currently, it's covered in a fine, downy hair called lanugo and a waxy coating called vernix. It has eyebrows, eyelashes, fingernails and toenails. It can hear and swallow. It can make its father feel completely alone.

When the postman comes I close my Internet window and go downstairs to retrieve the letters. Only one of them is for me. I separate the junk for recycling and put Lyd's in a pile that I intend to forward to her parent's address at the end of the week.

I open mine.

The cover letter is from a lawyer detailing how much I owe my publishing company (£14,654) and what my options are for repayment (very few). The next page is a receipt of monies owed and a breakdown of the coming interest and charges. The last page is a note from an account executive at the publishing house offering me the opportunity to buy the remaining stock of my books at a reduced rate (from as little as £2.16 per unit for all 1,278 units, ranging up to £3.91 per unit, for a minimum of 10 units). I'm still reading the final page of the letter when someone knocks on the door.

I look through the frosted glass and see that it's Jayne, Lyd's sister, so I run into the kitchen and hide behind the breakfast counter. When the knocking returns I wonder what I'm doing, why I've panicked, and since I've acknowledged the fact that I'm squirming by the counter I tell myself that I have to walk through the hall and face her. I can't plead temporary insanity. I'm a coward if I don't go.

I open the front door to a blast of brightness, Jayne's silhouette and a loud burst of birdsong. The discordant melodies are so loud that they almost seem to be connected to the sunlight. They throb in my eyes and brain in the same way. I try to focus on Jayne.

"This is unexpected," I say, squinting, my right eye twitching all of a sudden. "Come in."

"Have you just got up? I could come back after work?"

She glances down at my hand. I look at it too. I'm scrunching up the letter in my fist. I manage to angle it so she can't see the letterhead but my fist has given off a general air of tension.

"I've been up for hours," I say. "I just like working in my dressing gown."

"Okay. Sure."

She steps into the hall. She's wearing a sixties-style paisley dress, cherry red Dr Martens and purple tights with white polka dots. She doesn't have much in common with Lyd (on any level) but in their physical forms I always register a resemblance around the neck and shoulders, and they both have the same curves on their legs. These simple lines, these echoes of Lyd, make me want to reach out and hold her, embrace her, but I have enough clarity of mind to know that only a desperately lonely man would do that.

"Do you want a drink? Tea? Coffee? Juice?" I ask, closing the front door and walking towards the kitchen.

She follows me.

"Maybe a glass of water," she says.

I quickly stash my disturbing letter behind the fruit bowl on the way past and then pour her a glass of filtered water from the fridge.

"How's it going?" she asks, glancing at the fruit bowl.

"I miss her."

Jayne nods and meets my eyes sympathetically, mirroring my sorrow as she accepts her glass of water. My right eye twitches and I wonder if she sees it.

"It must be hard," she says.

"We should be together. Preparing for the baby."

My eye twitches again. Jayne breaks eye contact and moves away from me. I'm pretty sure she's seen my eyeball juddering around in its socket and is going to phone Lyd the second she leaves to tell her that I've gone completely mad.

"How's the writing?" she asks.

"My book? Good. I'm over half way through the first draft now. It's getting there, slowly but surely."

"I do wonder about creative people; where it all comes from."

"Anyone could do it. Honestly. It's nothing special."

"I imagine it's a very spiritual experience, writing a book."

"People think writers are creative authorities who work up in the castle but really we're just fools prattling around in the village. We spend our days chasing imaginary people, misinterpreting messages, doing dull chores. Have you read *The Castle*?"

She shakes her head.

"It's good that you're keeping on top of it," she says. "With everything that's going on."

"I feel like, maybe, if I write a good book it might prove to Lyd that I'm on the right track. She'll know I haven't lost it."

"I don't think she'd care if you wrote a masterpiece."

"Probably not."

A tapping sound comes from the sliding door. My face jolts towards the noise. It's Blackie, drumming his beak against the glass. My right eyeball flutters and my stomach turns. Jayne looks over, with normal curiosity. An unsettling sense of being watched comes over me. I feel exposed. I can faintly hear the birdsong on the other side of the glass.

"Oh, yes, that's right," she says. "Lydia told me about this little guy. Doesn't he come for his breakfast or something?"

She walks towards the sliding door and Blackie flies away, back onto the lawn.

"Sometimes."

"Look at his little kiddies badgering him. They're almost as big as he is."

I go to the cupboard, grab a handful of sultanas, pull the sliding door across and throw them out onto the lawn. Birdsong floods into the kitchen. Most of the birds fly up onto the fence or on top of the evergreen. Blackie stays on the lawn, quickly takes the opportunity to eat a couple of sultanas and then adds to the whistling rumpus:

– *chink-chink, chook-chook, chink-chink, chook-chook* –

(*She can see your eye twitching.*)

I quickly slide the door shut and turn my back to the garden. Jayne watches as the birds all fly back down onto the grass. My right eye is now twitching more than it's still.

"Look at him feeding them all. Why can't they just pick up the raisins themselves?"

"Sultanas," I say.

"Do they always have so many chicks?"

"No. They usually just have two or three but a cat got the female from another nest so the male moved on. This one looks after their chicks as well as his own."

"Aw, that's sweet."

"He looks after his people."

Jayne turns towards me.

"You know, she's miserable without you."

"*Really?*"

"You don't have to sound so happy about it."

"Sorry," I say, rubbing my eye. "It's just… she left."

"Yes. She left. But she could have kicked you out."

"Do you think that means something?"

"Yes. Of course. Even if *she's* too stubborn to admit it."

"You think I have a chance?"

"Definitely."

"What should I do? I don't dare call her. I don't dare do anything."

"You could start by taking your medication."

"That's not going to happen," I say, sighing.

"I know you think you stopped taking it for the right

139

reasons but this pregnancy has brought a lot up for Lydia. It's the worst possible time to try something like this."

I grab a small glass from the draining board, walk to the fridge and pour myself some orange juice.

"I think it's the best time," I say.

I close my eyes for a second whilst I put the juice back in the fridge and my back is turned to her, trying to relax, but my eyeball jitters around behind my eyelid.

"This is why you've ended up living on your own. You think you're doing this for Lyd and the baby but you're doing it for yourself. You're living on your own, you're writing your book instead of looking for work, you're not taking your medication, and you're doing all this because it's what *you* want. You're going to end up on your own completely but you don't see it."

"I see it. I do. But it's worth the risk. I don't want us to live in the shadows."

"Whatever that means."

"It's one of Lyd's phrases."

"Personally, I don't think she's ever really forgiven you for running off like that. Leaving her to deal with all that mess. This is just throwing it in her face."

"I know you're her sister, and I'm sorry to say it, but you don't know her like I do. And you don't know our situation, how it feels. She forgave me for all that. She had to, so we could grieve together. This is something else."

"Forgiving and forgetting are two different things."

I gulp down my juice, take the glass to the sink and look out the kitchen window. Blackie is still feeding his five pestering children. Jayne's right. He shouldn't have to feed them all. They're big enough to feed themselves. Why does he put up with it? Why does he let them twitter at him and bounce around him and make him do whatever they want? It's too stressful a sight. I have to turn my back to it.

"Vince... Do you have any plans?"

"When you look back at how she was when she was younger you all see the scientist in her, the high achiever, and that's good because you're proud of her, and you love the role she plays in your life, but she's not really like that. Not at heart. None of you see how deeply sensitive she is, how soft her humour is, how forgiving she is, how she always puts those she loves before herself. The decisions she makes reflect who she is, how she thinks and feels. We would have never got back together if she hadn't forgiven me."

I turn to face Jayne. She's looking at me, unsettled, because I'm resting the palm of my hand over my right eye. I'm not sure how long it's been there. I lower it and my eye starts twitching again. I screw up my cheek to try to stop it in its tracks but it doesn't work, it just makes me look like I'm pulling a strange face.

"You obviously don't want to talk about your plans. But we can talk about Lydia if you want. Why do *you* think she left?"

"I don't know."

"I want to help you, Vince. That's why I'm here. I think you're good for her. I think you're right for each other. You probably do know her better than I do. And with a baby on the way it makes sense for you to be together. But you have to face up to the reasons why she might have left you. You have to be willing to change."

"Into what?"

"I don't know. You know Lydia. She doesn't talk about this stuff. But decisions have to be made. You're living in a house she's paying for, for a start."

"Do you think you can get her to talk to me?"

"Do you really think you're ready?" she says. "No offence, but you need to do something with yourself."

"You mean get a job? That's all it ever comes down to for you lot."

"No. That's not what I meant. But since you brought it up: what if Lydia did stop supporting you? How would you afford your own place? How would you be a father if you had to separate? These should be eventualities you're preparing for. You have to be able to look after yourself. Otherwise, how will anyone think you can look after a child?"

"Charlie was happy and my life, the way I lived, was no different to how it is now."

"When Charlie was born your first novel had just been published and your writing career looked promising. Mum and Dad had helped you both get on the property ladder so you were cushioned from all of that. When it turned out your books weren't selling, Lydia's book suddenly made lots of money. So it made sense for you to stay at home and look after Charlie, because you could. Everything's changed since then. Lydia's quite well-off but you're back at the start again. Surely you see that?"

"I do. I know."

"You have to start looking after yourself or you're going to lose her."

I suddenly decide that I can't stand another second of this. I feel like my eye is going to explode. I approach Jayne, put one hand on her lower spine and the other on her shoulder and begin to usher her out of the house. Her eyes bulge with surprise but she accepts her fate without a challenge.

"Thanks for coming," I say. "I'm really going to think this through. I'll try harder. I promise."

I open the door for her. All the brightness and birdsong rushes in. I screw up my face and urge Jayne out onto the doorstep. She steps out. I'm just about to close the door on her when she turns around and says:

"Vince."

She's holding something out. Her glass of water. I take it from her.

"Look after yourself," she says. "Think about what I've said."

I close the door.

I should have stayed crouched by the breakfast counter.

After Jayne's visit I can't concentrate on writing or editing so I turn off my computer and draw blackbirds in my notebook to pass the time, trying not to think about the version of me that Jayne would be happy with. The first image is a terrible attempt at a realistic depiction, unmeasured and mutant. The second actually looks like a blackbird but it's more of a generic sketch. The third one is cartoonish and looks more like a crow.

It's a relieving change to watch the black ink from the nib of my fountain pen creating lines rather than words. The twenty-six letters of the alphabet seem so oppressive compared to the casual strokes a picture uses to gradually acquire its meaning. The hand moves more freely. The system is less restrictive.

I gradually start producing smaller and more emblematic images until I've developed a simple glyph. It's made up of two hooked and curved lines that give just the right impression. As I'm drawing these glyphs I start to hear Blackie up on the drainpipe. His whistle is entwining with the hooks and the curves of the lines. My mind is sinking and the symbols on the page are swelling and losing focus. I can't see the nib of my pen. My writing hand is shaking.

When Blackie releases a distinctive flurry of tweets a thought strikes me, true and bold. I rush to the baby's room, pull down the ladder and climb into the attic. The plastic white board is directly behind me, by the wall, covered by an old sheet. I grab the torch, fling off the sheet and illuminate Charlie's family portrait.

He depicted the house from the back, not the front. You can see this from the amount of wall that the doorway takes up. The sliding door is the entrance to inside. He was by no means a housebound child, we took him out all the time, but to him the outside world is the back garden.

The first figure is Mum. Her arms are a horizontal yellow line: love, acceptance. He has been very careful to give her a red smile.

The central figure is Charlie. He also has a red smile. His head is oversized, bigger than either of ours, and his body is a tiny lump. His arms are black: one pointing up at his mother, one pointing up at me.

I have a smile too but mine is black. I'm very tall. Relatively, Lyd could be my child. She's closer to his size. My arms are a purple diagonal line: one end points down towards him and the other up.

I follow the line of my arm up the image and there it is, the thing I'm looking for. I've stared at this portrait a hundred times and never made anything of it. Up on the top right corner of the house are two very small, very purposefully placed, hooked black lines. They are strikingly similar to my glyph. They represent a blackbird.

I stare at these two small, interlocking black hooks for three or four minutes. Did Charlie know about the blackbirds? Did Blackie speak to Charlie? Is Charlie speaking through Blackie? Is there a link? The picture provides no answers. It only adds weight to the creeping feeling that blackbirds are in control of my fate.

My contemplation is broken by the absence of solitude. There's something behind me. Eyes are on me. I know it's Charlie but I don't want to look. My heart is racing. My hands tingle and begin to sweat. I can feel his smile in the air around me. Almost hear his giggle.

I slowly turn around but, as I do, the feeling goes, the smile wanes. It's not Charlie. It's Blackie, standing in the middle of the floor. He doesn't move when I shine the torch on him. He must have got in through the cracked tile, the route the dead mother took to build her nest in here. His presence is filling me with dread. There is a plan and Blackie is a part of it. He opens his beak:

– *chink-chink, chook-chook, chink-chink, chook-chook* –

FIVE

Photons, the principal particles in electromagnetic fields, transmit electromagnetic radiation. A small frequency of this radiation is called the visible spectrum, or light (waves of which interact with retinas and amass into the sensation of sight). For this reason, photons are often referred to as "messenger particles". In laboratory settings, human exposure to certain frequencies of electromagnetic fields produces altered emotional states including fear, panic and disorientation, or relaxation, relief and contentment. Tests have also stimulated hallucinations and feelings of being watched, talked to or followed, in both malevolent and comforting contexts. This is to say, electromagnetic fields and their photons don't just affect what people see and believe, they are what people see and believe. Yet, their messages, when perceived, are not necessarily aligned with the objective truth. Subtle fluctuations in a brain's electromagnetic field changes the way the photons' "reality message" is received and interpreted.

Lyd's standing in our doorway with a lonely and angry look on her face. It's the day of the anomaly scan and she's come to pick me up. She's wearing a yellow-green chiffon maternity dress and, despite her despondent mood, she's glowing and looks beautiful. Her life-forming, five-month bulge makes me feel like I'm emerging from a world where nothing real grows.

"You look rough," she says. "Have you lost weight?"

"It was the medication, bloating me up. I'm slowly getting back to my old shape. Do you want to come in for a minute?"

"No."

"Okay."

I follow her out to the car, ignoring the birdsong in the air and Blackie on the telephone wire across the road.

It's all under control, I tell myself, as I get in the passenger seat. *Act normal, don't freak out and everything's going to be fine.*

The fact that Jayne created this opportunity doesn't necessarily render it meaningless. There's a slim chance Lyd could be ready, piece by piece, to let me back into her life. Of course, she might want nothing to do with me but think that I deserve to be part of the major moments in our child's development. Whatever the answer, I don't want to get off on the wrong foot. As Lyd drives I move over safe ground and don't mention the fact that I've got a feeling we're being followed by the red car behind us.

She's been out to the Large Hadron Collider in Geneva doing freelance work for CERN (she's been going once or twice a year since the second year of her PhD). She loves it there (it's her only chance to get away from numbers and do some "real engineering") so I stay conscientiously quiet and coax her into talking about her trip. I manage almost five minutes before making a huge blunder.

"It felt strange," I say, "not quite knowing if you were away or not. We've never been apart like that."

She glances at me harshly and then looks back at the road with amused disbelief.

"That's funny," she says, "because I have a distinct memory of planning a child's funeral without quite knowing where you were."

Again, it's that skill I have for drawing attention to exactly the wrong thing. We drive in silence for a few minutes.

146

"So was there anything interesting at this conference you mentioned?" I ask. "After Geneva?"

"I went to see an astronaut speak," she says.

I wipe my palms on my thighs and look over my shoulder through the rear windscreen. The red car is still behind us. The driver is a shadowy blur.

"An astronaut?"

"Really charismatic for an American guy."

"Uh-huh."

"It was supposed to be a respite in the schedule, something non-taxing in the middle of all the serious science, but he ended up getting the majority of the press."

"How come?" I ask, watching the red car turn right in the side mirror.

"He was speaking about his perspective after being up in space so many times. Mostly the reformed environmentalist stuff you'd expect – beautiful blue ball, terrible wars, pointless borders, reckless use of resources, all that. Obviously, being American, he didn't politicise any of his views, he just kept talking about now being the time to act, but he did have a couple of interesting ideas."

"For example?"

"Like, in the twenty first century, Western children grow up with interactive, digital images of Earth at their fingertips and, whilst they're barely beyond the mirror stage before most of them have met people outside the family, a lot of them are self-identifying as citizens of a planet floating in space. For the first time, a toddler's conception of the world is finite. Earth is their home. He thinks this is an unprecedented conceptual upheaval that will change the way future generations will come to think of their identity and where they live."

"There's only one place a toddler really knows about," I say, "the centre of the universe."

My witticism doesn't even earn me a grin and, under the circumstances, I felt like I'd done spectacularly well.

Lyd continues talking as though I'm not really involved in the conversation.

"He was quite eloquent about how the sky isn't a limitless expanse and how, when seen from above, our atmosphere is a relatively thin collection of gases hugging the earth, protecting our entire ecosystem from the decimation of outer space, and how it's completely conceivable that we're changing the nature of this minuscule force-field by filling it with the wrong kinds of gases."

"Sounds like a soft-pot," I say, trying to amuse her again. "Don't they weed out the jelly brains in these astronaut programmes?"

She smiles this time, so quickly it could be a twitch. She doesn't want us to enjoy each other's company. She just wants to avoid talking properly by talking about this astronaut. Whilst this is relieving (because I don't want to have to lie about how I'm feeling and what I'm currently going through) it's also agonising because important things are purposefully going unsaid and our relationship feels all the more hopeless for it.

"I agree with most of what he said," she says, "any humanitarian does, but I want to know how such a sentimental subject can take centre stage at a supposedly world-renowned physics conference. The bottom line is that he's just another middle-aged man trying to validate his Messiah complex."

I quickly look over my shoulder. The road behind us is clear. There must be someone just slightly out of sight because I still feel like we're being followed.

"People eat that stuff up though, don't they? It appeases their guilt."

"The worst thing is that he's filled with awe by a nature that doesn't even exist. It's like watching a mushroom cloud rising over London and saying how beautiful it is. His perspective makes no attempt to deconstruct what's actually happing, or solve any real problems. Meanwhile people making breakthroughs in grand unification, superstring, inflationary cosmology – breakthroughs that will change the way we understand the universe forever – they're being ignored."

"You know, I'd still be looking at the world with seventeenth-century eyes if it wasn't for you."

She ignores this compliment and glances down at my lap. My hands are tightly gripping my thighs. I release them and try to find a relaxed stance but everything seems decentred and forced.

"His new-found respect for the planet is bullshit," says Lyd, more conviction behind her anger now. "He has absolutely no idea what's going on in the world, or how complicated its problems are. At a push he's, what, a glorified mechanic, a pilot? Who cares what he thinks or if he's had a vague, transcendental experience whilst sitting in a spaceship? He probably has a carbon footprint the size of Asia with all that rocket fuel and all those planes he takes to go and do his talks. And Eastern philosophy has been saying what he's saying for thousands of years. Maybe he should have just read a few books and become an environmental activist. It's such a naïve and pointless perspective."

My usual response to Lyd's anger would be to gently probe to see if there was something else upsetting her. This time, I simply nod in agreement because if there is something it's probably me.

"You're right," I say, massaging the back of my neck with my dank right hand. "Completely right."

We remain quiet for the rest of the journey. I try to sit as still as possible in order to attract no attention. I ban myself from looking in the mirrors. Nothing is following us, even if I feel it.

In the waiting room, twenty minutes after our appointment time, Lyd is still trying to get through a large bottle of mineral water. She's extremely tense. I'm looking around, reading the health posters on notice boards and jigging my right leg.

We're finally led into the ultrasound room by the same assistant as last time. The sonographer is different. She's a mole-faced woman with a big nose, tiny-screwed up eyes, wrinkled lips and greasy brown hair. Her voice has a nasal quality.

"Sit down, lie down, get your feet up," she says. "And pull that dress up. Let's have a look at you."

Lyd gets on the examination bed and hitches up her dress, resenting the speedy, matter-of-fact instructions because she thinks most medical professionals are sadists and that stripping people of their dignity and confidence is all part of a game they pretend they're not playing.

The sonographer starts moving fast and explaining little. Within moments Lyd's bulging stomach is covered in gel and the mole-woman is racing through a series of checks and measurements without explaining a single thing to us.

"If you're thinking of finding out the sex today you can forget it," she says. "Little blighter has its legs crossed."

"Oh," says Lyd, trying to sound disappointed instead of antagonistic.

"Maybe we could wait a couple of minutes?" I suggest.

"Could be two minutes, could be two weeks but I haven't got time to find out," says the sonographer. "Behind schedule as it is."

"We know," says Lyd.

Again, the sonographer sets off on a series of nozzle twists and writes little encoded notes on a form that I'm sneaking glances at but can't decipher.

"There's not much point getting a sonogram either," she says. "It's in a funny position. You won't be able to see the face."

"But you can tell if everything's okay?" says Lyd. "It looks fuzzy. Why is it so fuzzy?"

"Everything's fine… Fine, fine, fine. You can book again if you really want a clearer picture."

"*What's that?*" I ask.

My anxious tone peaks Lyd's interest. She looks at the screen and tries to see what I'm seeing.

"What's what?" asks the sonographer, eager to get through this as quickly as possible.

"That," I say, pointing at the top half of the screen.

"That's your baby," she replies.

Lyd's staring at me. My lower spine is trembling. I must be hallucinating. What I'm seeing can't be what I'm seeing because what I'm seeing isn't a baby. It's something else: some kind of deformed mutant, a disfigured runt, a grotesque homunculus. A wave of nausea rushes through me. A cold sweat quickly follows.

Not now, I'm thinking. *Not now.*

Lyd has a disgusted look on her face, like my existence is contaminating the air and making it unpleasant to breathe. I look around the room, increasingly dizzy, and see a small metal bin over in the corner. I run towards it and drop down onto my hands and knees.

For a second it seems like it's passed and I've just humiliated myself for nothing but when I look at the contents of the bin, at the disposed rubber gloves, paper towels and thin plastic condoms covered in lubricant, I'm suddenly dry heaving and retching. Deep undulations are curling through my spine and whipping out of my gullet. It's not real vomit, it's just air and drool, but it sounds harsh and insane.

SIX

In Plato's allegory of the cave, Socrates describes underground prisoners who are chained up facing a blank wall. Above, a procession of people and objects pass before a fire and their shadows project down onto this wall. Over time the prisoners give names to these shadows and come to accept them as real things. They become more and more skilled at perceiving them and predicting the order of their procession. When one of the prisoners is freed and sees the source of the shadows and the world above, he realises that his fellow prisoners will never believe that they are only looking at a puppet show and that the real world is above them. They will think that his eyes have been ruined, that he no longer sees the truth. Socrates argues that, by default, the free man now understands that the body is the real prison and that truth lies beyond the material world. He does not discuss what would have happened to the man if he went deeper into the cave.

I wake up late, thirsty, with a headache. There's a heat wave outside, trying to get in. My lithium tablets are on the bed. I fell asleep thinking about taking them again, feeling like I'd ruined everything.

Downstairs, Blackie is waiting for me at the sliding door. He pecks and pecks at it, trying to get my attention, but I ignore him. Birdsong is quietly bouncing off the walls and windows. I can't deal with any of it today so

I pull the blinds shut and go around the house closing all the curtains.

Staring at the living room ceiling, lying on the couch, I doze on and off all day, the house slowly warming through. I have no motivation to get up and I'm not tired enough to sleep. My consciousness weaves in and out of itself, hearing house noises and dream noises at the same time, neither here nor there, lost between spaces.

When it finally gets dark and the birds are asleep I feel a bit more awake. It occurs to me that Lyd might have contacted me via email. I go and check. She hasn't. After deleting my junk mail, the message from *CHARLIE* (Subject: (24) Re: direct contact…) pops back into the folder. I decide to write him another message and stare at the flashing cursor in the blank message box. I type, *Why are you doing this to me?* and the moment I press the key for the question mark the sound of tiny feet pitter-patters across the ceiling above me.

In the baby's room, I pull down the ladder. Looking up into the square of darkness, I no longer feel alone. As my head breaches the attic I smell the faint whiff of Charlie that permeates from all of his things. I turn on the torch, look around at his stuff and climb the rest of the way in. There's definitely somebody up here.

I step over the small box of Christmas decorations and hear shuffling behind the pile of boxes where I discovered the abandoned chicks. I approach the corner the boxes create and shine the torch down the slope of the roof. My stomach flutters as the beam of light passes over a physical object which twists and morphs, forming strange colours and bumps, until my eyes finally understand that it's a scrunched-up child: Charlie, sitting with his hands over his face. He's wearing red dungarees, a blue T-shirt with thin neon stripes running through it and a pair of blue shoes with red laces. It's the outfit he's wearing in my favourite photograph of him, the one I keep in my wallet.

"Who are you hiding from?" I whisper.

When I speak he disappears and I hear running across the middle of the floor behind me. I follow the direction of the sound, slowly navigate the floor space with the torch pointing ahead of me and eventually find him again, this time beneath the wardrobe doors that are leaning against the sidewall.

When the light of the torch passes over his face he wriggles with excitement.

"Charlie? Why are you hiding?" I ask.

He disappears again and, behind me, I hear the sound of his feet running across the middle of the floor. I realise that he might be playing hide-and-seek so this time I put on a mock-spooky voice, count down from ten and narrate my journey to find him.

Listening for audible clues, I hear him squirming and writhing over by his old cot so I dramatically lengthen the game, pivoting around his position and raising the tone of my voice until he makes a thrilled squeal, at which point I sweep the beam of the torch onto him and cry:

"Got you!"

Again, he disappears and I hear him running through the darkness.

We play like this for close to twenty minutes. There aren't all that many hiding spots but I know that his pleasure is mostly derived from the anticipation of waiting to be found so I try to make the build-up as tense and enjoyable as possible.

When I hear him behind the first pile of boxes again, I can't resist. It feels like he's really here, we're really playing this game. Hope has taken root in me so, instead of raising the volume of my voice and springing towards him, I kneel down in front of him. I still haven't seen his face. I have to see it but I daren't. I rest the beam of the torch on his chest and take a few breaths.

I desperately want to reach out and hold him. I inch the beam up to his neck, the dip of his chin, but there's no face, just blackness, death; a small black shadow scurries towards a crack in a roof tile and disappears. The attic is empty. I'm alone. There's no running sound in the darkness. I sit in the attic for hours, just in case, but he doesn't come back.

On the couch, it's getting light and I can't sleep. I'm haunted by his absence. Every time I get close to nodding off I hear him in the distance – a giggle, a squeal, running feet. I need him. More than ever. I can't let go.

Hours? Days? All I know is that the heat wave continues, ignoring the closed curtains, moving through every object in the house, into every tiny space and crevice. I idle around – lying on the couch, leaning against walls, getting warmer, sweating, drinking water, questioning why I saw Charlie, thinking about why I want to see him again so much, wondering how the birdsong is getting through the walls and into my ears. Every peek through the curtains reveals a blackbird conspicuously close to the house. Now and again I hear the clicking sound of a beak pecking on the sliding door in the kitchen.

Outside is pure bombardment: light, heat, birdsong, blackbirds, huge buildings, millions of people, sweat, garbage, technology, decay, carbon dioxide, pot holes, chewing gum, coffee shops, pushchairs, mobile phones, double-decker buses, advertisements, cars, traffic lights, lamp posts, paving stones, tarmac, double yellow lines, clothing, faces, hair, train tracks, tunnels, barriers. Everything is unnaturally connected; welded, wired, waged. It's all too much.

Inside, I might have a chance. Me and the house have a long-standing mutual dependency. Here, I'm not just a lost and hopeless man living in his partner's house, I'm in a safe place, fighting to get through a dark time, taking an isolated opportunity to try to come to terms with some of the blind spots in my mind. If I stay here everything might work out. I just have to avoid going outside, where everything's connected, where they'll see that I'm not part of it all.

I sweat. I drink water. The couch becomes slightly moist. Darkness falls and rises. Birdsong quietens and swells. Distant traffic and plug sockets hum. Heat clings to everything. Time is completely unpunctuated until I finally hear the faint sound of scurrying in the attic. I stand up but have to stay still for thirty seconds while the blood rushes into my head and out again.

When I get up there Charlie is sitting in plain sight. He isn't trying to hide from the beam of my torch. I can see his face. He's smiling, glad to see me, wearing those red dungarees again. I drop to my knees and release a mournful groan. Emptiness and sadness twist in my guts. He begins to fade out of sight so I fight my feelings, rock my spine, clench my gut, rein everything back and force it down. When I'm done he's still sitting there.

"Do you want Daddy to read you a story?" I ask, almost whimpering.

"No," he says, definite, shaking his head.

The presence of this word, the reality of it, shocks me. I didn't expect him to speak. Last time his movement made noises and he made a few reactionary sounds but it all lacked the immediacy of an independent mind choosing a word and projecting it at me. It could have all been in my head. But hearing him. Hearing his voice. It makes me see that he's really here. He has wants and needs and I don't know what they are.

"Do you want to play with your cars?"

"Make pictures," he says.

My hands shake as I scramble through a couple of boxes, trying to remember which one his crayons and felt-tip pens are in. I eventually find them on top of some books underneath lots of his drawings and paintings.

There's no paper so I rush down the ladder to the printer in my office. As I grab a few sheets I have a morbid moment of self-reflection where I imagine the pain of rushing up into an empty attic but he's still there waiting patiently when I get back.

I put the blank pieces of paper in front of him and he

begins scribbling. Lines and colours form on the page and I follow their appearance keenly, pointing the torch at the emerging picture so he can see.

I forgot how intensely honest and creative he is. There is no pause for thought in his drawing and colouring, no doubt or reflection. He is lost in the process. Not a single moment is wasted worrying about how his image will be perceived. This is art as id, image as dream, self as symbol, and it's untainted by creative block, lack of focus or the pursuit of value.

When he is done he grabs the corner of the page and, without checking the image over, knowing that it is exactly as he intended, holds it out for me.

"Look," he says.

I take the page from him and inspect it. It is a version of Lyd in stick man form. Her arms are open. Her big face is smiling. A large messy block of yellow starts in her belly and almost takes over the whole page. Above her there is a black scribble in the sky. Below there are green lines and a pair of hooked black lines.

"Is this Mummy?" I ask.

He nods but he isn't looking at me. He's busy drawing the next picture. It takes him a long time to finish. It's another picture of Lyd. This time he only uses black. Lyd's mouth is sad. Blackness is protruding from her stomach.

"This one's not very happy, is it? Is there something wrong with Mummy?"

"Yes," he says, nodding his head.

"Is she sad?"

He shakes his head.

"Is she poorly?"

He shakes his head again.

"What is it then?"

"Mummy doesn't love Charlie," he says.

"Of course she does."

"Mummy loves baby, not Charlie."

"That's a horrible thing to say."

"Baby's going to die," he says.

"Please, Charlie. Don't say that."

"Baby's going to die."

"Charlie, no," I say, reaching for his shoulders.

The second I reach for him he doesn't exist. His shoulders aren't there. His felt-tip pens and crayons are scattered around on top of blank pieces of paper. There are no drawings anywhere. The pictures have gone. He's taken them with him. I think I hear a little scratching sound behind a pile of boxes but when I look there's nothing there.

The house is too hot. Outside is still impossible. The only thing that matters to me is seeing Charlie again. I decide to move up into the attic. This way, whenever he's around, I'll be there to see him straight away. I won't miss a moment.

I take up an extension cable, plug in a small lamp and fashion a makeshift bed. I empty all the bottles I can find and fill them with water. I even fetch the mop bucket and bleach so I won't need to visit the toilet more than once a day.

After putting all the tinned food that doesn't need cooking in a bag I notice a yellow Post-It note at the back of the cupboard: *If you can read this we need more food xxx*. It jars me for a second. I forgot about Lyd's notes. I close the cupboard door with a flinch.

When I'm all set up I feel safe. There are no windows for blackbirds to tap on and, although I can still hear it, the birdsong is quieter up here. Time – or its overabundance – is the only problem. The hours are long and uninterrupted. There's no night or day. It's endless.

Ten hours? Fifteen? There's still no sign of him and my eyes are worn out so I quickly go downstairs and retrieve the stopwatch I sometimes use to time myself when I go jogging. It makes sense to rest in short bursts because, if I spread my sleeping out throughout the day, there's a greater probability that I won't miss him entirely. I use the stopwatch as an alarm and trial sleeping for half an hour and then staying awake for three hours.

After three, maybe four rounds of this I struggle to stay awake for the full three hours so I have to keep reducing the sleeping and waking times. It gets blurrier and blurrier but I eventually find a good balance sleeping for three minutes and waking for ten.

Meals are reduced to sporadic grazing. I'm never hungry but now and then I notice a strange twinge in my stomach and eat a couple of sultanas. After a single bowel movement my digestive system slows down to a near stop. I only have to go down to empty the mop bucket into the toilet once. The light level surprises me. The edges of the blinds gleam and lint collides with golden photons slipping through into the room. The whole house is thick with warmth.

It's hard to know if he's ever going to show up again but occasionally I wake and sense that he's been and I've missed him, or else that he's getting close but choosing to stay absent. This makes me feel so empty that my stomach cramps and folds me in half.

More and more I find myself crying. Occasionally, my nervous system is attacked by electric convulsions. My back arches, my limbs tense up and the back of my head slides around on the floor, banging into cardboard boxes. My spine is constantly shaking near the pelvis. My hands shiver. My right eye twitches. Sweat drips off my back. The air gets thicker and thicker. I'm awake, I'm asleep, I'm awake, I'm asleep.

Soon enough my attention is not so much focused on seeing Charlie but on feeling his presence in the space. I have to make myself ready to receive him. It's a process. The first two were flukes. All the conditions were accidentally right. Now I have to work for it.

Everything changes when he's near. When he's close by I lie back and try to feel him washing through me, try to summon him through my body. I have no appetite for anything else. This feeling is the only thing I'm hungry for.

When he finally appears weeks might have passed, months, but it's as if he's come from nowhere, as if I've put in absolutely no effort and he was always going to simply show up at this moment. This is the fated time. I should have known all along.

"Charlie?"

He ignores me.

"Charlie?"

He starts grinning. He's playing the ignoring game. My tension subsides.

"Do you want to play a game?" I ask him.

He's still trying to win at the ignoring game.

"Charlie. You're terrible at ignoring. I can see you grinning."

He laughs and looks at me.

"Is that what you want to play? The ignoring game."

He shakes his head and looks around.

"Fire Engines on the Moon," he says.

"We can't play that one. There is no moon."

"*Daddy*. Please. Fire Engines on the Moon."

"Okay," I say. "Don't go anywhere. I have to get some things."

I rush downstairs and get two cushions from the living room, then string, paper, Sellotape and lots of old newspapers. Charlie is still there when I get back and sits dutifully by my side, marvelling at my handcraft. It takes me almost an hour to make but I recall the process of creating the first moon very clearly.

When the final piece of paper is attached, I remember one last thing and so descend the ladders into the baby's room, remove the small hook from the ceiling, take it up to the attic and screw it into the highest roof beam. Charlie claps his hands together with glee when he sees the new moon hanging a foot from the attic floor.

"See? It's just like the old one."

"Please, Daddy. Fire engine," he says.

I open one of his boxes of toys, find his favourite fire engine and put it by his side.

"Do you want to see how the moon travels around the world?" I ask. "Or do you just want to play fire engines?"

"Yes," says Charlie, with a nod. "Moon Around the World."

"Sit there then."

I point to a spot on the floor and grab hold of the moon. Charlie shuffles into position with coy excitement, holding onto his fire engine.

"Close your eyes for a minute and imagine you're floating in space," I say. He closes them, his expression becoming slightly concerned. "You're the whole world, the big blue planet Earth, where we all live. Way over in the distance is the bright yellow sun. And that's what the world spins around all year long. Okay, you can open your eyes now. This, in my hand, is the moon—"

Charlie covers his face with his hands in excited anticipation.

"Not yet, Charlie. Wait for it."

He parts his fingers and looks through them with a smile.

"This is the moon. And when do we see the moon?"

Charlie mumbles.

"I can't hear you. When do we see the moon?"

"Night-time."

"That's right. We mostly see the moon at night time, when the sky is black. The sun shines onto it from the other side of the world and lights it up shiny and white. And what does the moon spin around?"

"Me," says Charlie, covering his eyes again.

"No, Charlie. What does the moon spin around?"

"Moon Around the World."

"That's right. And what are you?"

He giggles and hides his face in his lap.

"Charlie. What are you?"

He peeks up.

"World," he says.

"That's right," I say. "You're the world. And the moon goes around world… like this."

I push the moon in a small circle around Charlie and he laughs infectiously and intensely, like he almost can't bear how amused he is.

"See," I say, pushing it round. "The moon travels around the world."

After a few revolutions Charlie loses his timid fear, sits up and follows the moon's path with delighted eyes. Unconscious of his own wonderment, he raises his fire engine into the air as though it is caught up in the motion of it all. Occasionally, he releases a spasmodic burst of laughter.

His intense happiness is having a shimmering effect on my vision. Lamplight is passing through him. I can see the space behind him. My hands are sweating and beginning to shake so intensely that I can feel the reverberations in my elbows. I'm pushing a big white ball around an empty space. A toy fire engine is sitting still by my side.

The next time the moon comes around I clutch it in my jittery hands, hold it to my chest, tuck my chin down into it and stare at the empty space where he was, trying – but failing – to will him back into existence. I don't ever want to let it go.

"I won't," I promise the warm air all around me. "I won't."

SEVEN

A black hole's entropy is proportional to the size of its event horizon, not its inner volume. Since a black hole is space in a state of maximum entropy, this can be taken to mean that there is an elemental spatial entity – a region of space that allows for one unit of entropy – and that this space is a surface area, not a volume. To put it another way, it might reveal that the universe works in a similar way to a hologram. If true, a physical, linear existence in space and time is a false construct. Every moment, from the beginning of the universe to the end, already exists on a flat surface, surrounded by inconceivable dimensions. Time is a circle, space is an illusion and reality is relative to the number of dimensions that something exists in.

I'm standing on Suicide Bridge, my eyes tracing the skyline. The rumble of speeding traffic rises from below. London is cloaked in fumes and heat. The city is a single thing, a single word, a single idea. It has survived plague, fire, bombs, war. It's over two thousand years old. I'm not even a speck of dust falling off its skin. I grip the bridge's black metal bars. My legs are agitating. Someone pulls up beside me on a vintage pushbike. An unnecessarily enhanced startle reflex passes through my body.

"Don't do it," says the cyclist, mock-seriously.

In a petrified stupor, staring at the sunlight in his ginger beard and the sweat glistening on his freckled skin, the attributes of the stranger slowly form a memory of words:

Dieter, bookshop, barge, mushrooms. With them, his flat, meaningless face takes on form and character.

"No. Never. Good. Hi, Dieter. Hi."

"I didn't take you for a jogger. I almost didn't recognise you. I can't stand it. Bores the hell out of me."

He's talking about my clothes. I put on my jogging outfit because I wanted to be invisible. I wanted people to see a jogger, not me. Dieter saw me anyway.

"All that time in the cave," I say. "No movement."

"I don't know how you do it. I'd go out of my mind, cooped up on my own all day... I'm not disturbing a profound moment here, am I?"

"No. Far from it."

"Good."

"It's all surface. It looks real but it's just memories piled on top of each other."

"Okay."

"Lyd was right. It's best to keep the door shut. Keep the cat in the box."

I let go of the bars and look at Dieter. He's looking down the street beyond me. His cheeks are bunched up and his squinting eyes are awkwardly imagining his own back, cycling away.

"How's the mushroom farm coming along?" I ask.

"Erm, yeah... I'm still at the bookshop at the moment. Can't get the funds together. My mate in Wales wants me to partner up with him. It's the only place where there's a real mushroom scene at the moment."

"Sure."

"But I'm in a really serious relationship with my yoga teacher. And I don't want to sell my barge. How's the writing going?"

"I'm trying not to force it. Wait. Listen. See what comes. Don't judge it."

"Are you writing another novel then?" he asks, looking out at the view.

"Stories about delusions... Different times. Different places."

"Sounds interesting. Can you believe this weather? Best summer we've had in years."

"You don't want to sell your boat?"

"Barge. No. But I can't get it to Wales. And this yoga teacher..."

"You have to learn how to hear the surface. Stop hearing too much. You know? Just hear her."

"I'd love to wax lyrical about her, really, but I have to get to work."

"Sure."

"See you later."

He cycles off. I start jogging. Blackie swoops down and lands on the end of Suicide Bridge. I stop before him, waiting for a message or instruction but he just wants to demonstrate his power for a moment. He flies up onto the roof of the first house and whistles diagonally across the road. Over there, the way he calls, another Blackie acknowledges him and tweets further down the road to another Blackie who's standing on a lamppost at the crossroad ahead. I set off jogging again and as I pass each bird it chirps to the next one:

– *tck-tck-tck-tck-tck-tck* –

(*Keep watching him. It's nearly time.*)

Blackbirds talk about me all the way to Hampstead Heath. Every time I think I might be imagining it another one is looking at me, whistling to the next one. The park is full of people. The sight of them is overwhelming, almost too much. Their flat, desperate souls are jumping out of their eyes. I stick to the paths through the woods and stay away from Parliament Hill and the main fields so that I don't come across any crowds. I have a bench in mind that I want to sit on – over by the boating pond – but first I want to run the lap I used to walk with Charlie.

As I speed along by the playground I find myself slowing down and standing still, watching the children and their parents. I'm aware of how I might look – that I live in an era where I can't glance at a child without its paranoid parents thinking that I want to sexually abuse and kill it – but Charlie loved coming here with me. I used to be one of those parents, beyond the gates.

There are twenty-three children on the playground, eleven parents and four pushchairs lined up against the perimeter. One girl in a yellow-and-white polka dot dress is screaming on the swings so loudly that it's beginning to embarrass her mother. I quickly make all the connections between the parents and the children. Two boys are here with a man text-messaging on a bench (he keeps glancing at them). Four of the bigger girls, about nine or ten years old, are the children of three women standing together over by the monkey bars. One rogue girl and boy are here alone. Of them all, only one boy is unaccounted for. He's sitting in the box compartment the children go into before crossing the blue rope bridge. He's sad, morbid, hiding on his own. He's not playing with anyone, not talking. Nobody's checking on him or looking for him. He doesn't look like a boy who would be left to roam free. Even from this distance I can see that his haircut is more expensive than mine.

I'm getting increasingly worried about this little boy. My legs are jiggling. The birdsong is getting loud and intrusive, swelling out from the surrounding trees. I pointlessly wipe my damp hands across my sweaty face. He's only three or four. He shouldn't be left unattended. Maybe his mum or dad popped out to get him an ice cream, or get themselves a coffee.

Maybe I'm his mum or dad, I think, and then sneer.

I decide I better stay here and look out for him in the meanwhile, just in case.

The group of three mums over by the monkey bars start glancing over at me. I jump three times, bringing my knees right up to my chest. I can't stand still. One of the mothers is particularly unsubtle. At the precise moment she covertly points at me, a child's hand clasps tightly around the index finger of my right hand, the way Charlie used to hold it. She thinks I'm a demented paedophile who has just stolen a child.

I look down but Charlie's not there. When I look back at the playground I can't see the four-year-old boy. I scan all the places he could be. One of the fathers has joined the three worried mothers by the monkey bars and is looking my way. My rising panic tells me that they will think I'm crazy if I try to warn them about the child who just went missing. I should just start jogging, look like a jogger.

Before I set off I look around for a sign and, sure enough, Blackie's standing on the backrest of the nearest bench, watching me, waiting. If I sit there, it's near enough to show that I'm not fleeing and it faces away from the playground and so displays that I'm not predisposed to constantly look at children. I head towards it.

– *tck-tck-tck-tck-tck-tck* –

(*We're watching. Everybody's watching.*)

Blackie flies away as I approach.

Sitting on the bench, I take a sip of my water and then spread my arms out. I wait seventeen seconds before I twist my neck to glance at my accusers. They're all looking in another direction now. I follow the line of their stares and see a man who is wearing the same shorts and t-shirt as me. He is walking away from them. A four-year-old boy is holding his index finger. It's the boy from the playground.

The man standing with the three mothers breaks away from them to use his mobile phone. From his urgency, and the way he keeps eyeing the man and the boy, it seems like he's calling the police.

I stand on the bench, trying to glean more of the scene, and start waving my arms around. I'm trying to get their attention and show them that the man with the boy and me are different people, but they won't look. They're too intently focused on them.

"It's not me!" I find myself shouting. "My boy's dead!"

A happy family who are out to walk two golden retrievers and grandma in her wheelchair are talking about me, glancing, staring. The birdsong is getting louder again. Twittering chaos flitters through the air. I hop off the bench and start running away from the playground.

I must be running too fast because people are looking at me like a criminal. I slow down and jog over to the boating lake trying to avoid people's eyes, trying to jog like a jogger.

An old man is sitting on the bench I planned to sit on. He has a Jack Russell on his lap. The bench before him is free, as is the one further along, but I sit next to him anyway. It could be a sign. I might have to talk to him.

As I sit down his dog immediately erupts into a whirl of barking and spinning. The man looks at me sidelong, well aware that the other benches nearby are free, and pins his dog down onto his lap, reassuring it with whispers.

"My little boy's dead," I say. "He used to smile when I whispered in his ear. Astrocytoma. If you could tell your dog one thing what would it be?"

I reach towards his lap to stroke the Jack Russell. It growls and its flews tremble. I snap my hand back. The old man shoos it off his lap. At first the dog looks back at him with its tail raised, waiting to see if he is about to stand, but with no movement or instructions from its master it decides to run after a goose about fifty metres away on the grass behind us.

"Merdre," says the old man.

I'm only half sure that this is the word he says. It could have been a dismissive and inaudible grumble. It's not likely that he used a made-up word from the *Ubu* trilogy that has the double connotation of "shit" and "murder". Nonetheless, I decide to move forward as though this is the word he's uttered.

"Sure, sure. *Ubu Roi*. The realm beyond metaphysics. A dog would get that."

"My little dog's dead," says the old man.

I look over my shoulder. I can't see it anywhere.

"Sure, sure," I say, my legs bouncing up and down four and a half times a second. "Dead. I don't think so. What else would you tell him?"

"Life is plentiful," he says, "but cheap."

"A literary theme. Nineteenth-century Russian realism. Twentieth-century Southern Renaissance. I never got to read a decent book with Charlie."

"Dead."

"Sure. Sure. Your dog's dead. Do you hear all that birdsong?"

The old man looks up at the empty sky, screwing his face up. I close my eyes and wiggle my fingers about, trying to capture the cadence of the sound.

"Ubu!" the old man shouts. "Ubu!"

His Jack Russell is running back towards him. He's standing up to leave. When he looks back at me he has a different face. I try to ignore this and look at the bright squiggles of light drifting along the surface of the water on the boating pond. After a couple of minutes everything I look at drifts sideways in both directions. The world is just a surface. Everything that connects up and down, left and right, forwards and backwards, is just random nonsense that easily comes undone.

I'm lost in golden light and birdsong, everything twittering and unreal, when a muscly gym freak with tribal tattoos and a head like a rock tears through my world with an angry voice. He's shouting into his mobile phone. I can't hear the words but I find his anger fascinating. I stand up and start following him.

His vest has the slogan *I could bench you* on the back. His neck and both wrists have chunky silver chains hanging around them. He's holding a rope that could be a dog's lead but there's no dog. He walks with a swagger (it's unclear if he does this because of the nature of his bulk or because he wants to possess as much space as possible).

Once he enters a path through the woods and puts his phone back into his pocket I walk fast and catch him up. Now that we are beneath the trees the birdsong is even louder.

"Why are you so angry?"

"Get fucked, bro," he says, mildly startled by my sudden appearance. "I'm seriously not in the mood for a whack job today."

I look up into the nearest tree. Blackie's up there, looking down. The giant demented song is all around me, becoming noisier and more confounding.

"Sure. Sure. Sure," I say, speaking louder so that I can hear myself over all the noise. "But was there even anyone on the other end? Does it matter? Where's your dog?"

"Get the fuck away from me, yeah?"

He shoves me away. I almost fall but keep my balance. He's marching away. His vest now says *Blackbirds protect you* so I spring back towards him.

"Sure. Sure. Sure," I say. "Pure, unmotivated, irrational violence: the unifying element in all mankind. Inescapable aggression until the end of time."

He stops, raises his head to the sky and turns back towards me wrapping the rope for his non-existent dog around his fist.

"Listen, psycho. I'm gonna snap you in two if you don't stop following me. Get me?"

He walks on.

"You're the boss," I say, continuing to shadow him.

He tries to speed up but I'm quick on his heels. He stops and turns, stamping down his left foot and raising his right fist.

"Have you got a death wish or summink, bro?"

"Now, Blackie," I cry into to the trees. "Attack!"

He ducks his head with a slight flinch and slowly looks up to where Blackie is standing on a tree branch. He sees nothing of note. The anger in his face disperses into exasperated disbelief.

"Last chance, nutjob. I mean it. Wrong guy. Wrong day."

He lowers his fist and carries on walking. I'm quick to his shoulder.

"Sure, sure, sure. Maybe you're grieving. Anger is part of that. Maybe your dog died and this is our big cosmic coincidence that's going to create a perfect collision of meaning."

He pivots towards me. A powerful right hook smashes into the side of my head. Everything goes black. I fall to the ground. A huge thudding pain begins to throb on the side of my head and in half of my brain. A foot slams into my gut.

"You don't know when to quit, do you?"

Crimson drool connects me to the floor. London's subterranean world vibrates through the liquid strand, ancient and overloaded.

Another kick, this time the toe of his running shoe flies piercing into the left side of my ribcage. A squealing wheeze involuntarily surges through my throat.

"Sick fuck," he says. "You wanted this."

I roll onto my back.

Four or five more kicks. I loose count. Kidney, ribs, shoulder, neck, ribs. I'm in foetal position after the second, trying to protect my head. I feel swells of pain that could be kicks but might just be aftershocks bouncing through my body.

His rage is quelled once I'm limp. He spits on the ground next to me and walks away. I catch a glimpse of the rope he's carrying, hanging like a noose.

"I thought you were protecting me," I mumble, incoherently.

– *tck-tck-tck-tck-tck-tck* –

(*He's ready.*)

My mouth is filling up with saliva that tastes of copper. Everything looks different when I close my eyes. My pain has patterns, symmetries. I can see it. A woman asks if I'm alright, if I need any help.

"Pain is terrible," I mutter.

She repeats herself.

I shake my head and hold my hand out, implying that I don't want her to do anything. She walks away, looking back at me, taking out her mobile phone. This brings me back into a more present state. I remember that there are eyes everywhere. If they see me like this they'll take me away, lock me up, force-feed me chemicals.

I manage to lurch onto the grass verge and crawl far enough into the trees that people on the path can't see me. It's cooler here, but darker. The musky scent of insect life is in my nostrils. My skin itches. My face bleeds slowly. Birdsong stabs at my ears. I can't see any birds.

I struggle to sit up, my back against a tree trunk. My spine jars against the hard nubs and wrinkles. Tiny, silent midges float around like hyperactive lint. A grey squirrel scurries up a distant tree. My right eye slowly swells shut. The birdsong reverberates with the pain in my head, a migraine made of tinnitus.

It's been such a hot summer that the leaves are all limp and lifeless. These floppy edges have created lots of little gaps where thin shards of sunlight shoot down to the undergrowth. I pass a hand through the warmth of a couple of them and, as I do this, Blackie swoops down and lands on the toe of my right running shoe.

He jumps and turns one hundred and eighty degrees and all the foliage behind him blurs and turns into a gold-and-green blur. He jumps and turns one hundred and eighty degrees again and I see faces everywhere, evil green faces made out of leaves, flat, monstrous, screaming in agony.

Blackie jumps to face me, still perched on my right foot, both yellow-ringed eyes looking at me. His bill opens. I can see down his throat. A message is coming from inside him, from the deep beyond. It pierces my skull and splits through my brain:

Nothing is connected.

An intense electric pain rips through my nervous system. I hold my head and close my eyes. The pain crashes and explodes, smashing around in chaotic clusters. I writhe and twist. My body judders and flinches, jerks spasmodically. I weep. Twitch. Flinch. Gravity is crushing me. I'm falling. Everything is broken. Everything I care about is gone. There's nothing left. The despair is bottomless.

THIRD
TRIMESTER

ONE

Many of the unification theories in scientific discourse accept the universe as a series of inevitable occurrences caused by the underlying laws of nature and the initial conditions of life. In this sense, science's crowning achievement, its theory of everything, might merely add credence to one of humanity's most ancient ideas: that the universe is governed by the principle of fate. If true, people will come to see their lives as part of a grand cosmological equation, predetermined by the initial conditions on the tip of time's arrow. Questions about the nature of freewill would be resigned to history but the feeling of freedom would continue to confound.

I spend the day slowly tidying up the attic and bringing all my things back down the ladder. My body is weak and sore. I have to take long rests between journeys. I feel lost and lonely, starved of contact with people and the world, afraid that things will never feel as connected or as meaningful as they once did.

Putting the cushions from the centre of the moon back on the couch, I receive a text message from Jamal asking me to pop over. Jamal never sends texts. Sometimes he doesn't even answer his front door when I'm knocking on it. His rare invitations always inspire a sensation of amused validation in me; being chosen by somebody who chooses so few. In this state, with my face swollen and bruised, my reality shaky and delicate, the pride aroused by this invitation rises through me with unexpected power. Jamal is suddenly the exact person I want to see. His message seems like a fated gift.

As always, Jamal answers his front door with an unlit joint hanging out of his mouth. His cautious, socially awkward eyes don't meet mine. He just stands aside and gestures for me to enter with a subtle smile on his face.

Inside, all the newspapers and engine parts are gone. The curtains are open. It almost looks like a normal person's house. The odours of oil and cannabis smoke still cling to the air, but not as intensely.

"Where's all your stuff?" I ask.

He shuts the front door.

"You've seen it like this before."

"No. I definitely haven't."

I walk into the centre of his living room and look around.

"I didn't even know you had a carpet."

"Shit, man," he says, catching sight of me. "What happened to your face?"

I touch my swollen eye gently.

"I tripped."

"Isn't that what victims of domestic abuse say?"

"This whole house used to be a victim of domestic abuse. What's going on?"

"I do this sometimes," he says, eyeing me quizzically. "I time it so all my projects end together, so I can cash in and focus on one big thing for a while. I take it you don't want to talk about it? It's okay. We don't have to."

"We'll get to the bruises. Give me a chance."

"Sorry. Your face is a real mess though."

"I've definitely never seen your house like this," I say, forcing the shift.

"You have."

"I haven't. It's so tidy."

"Come on," he says, frowning at my bruises and forcing himself not to mention them again. "I want to show you something."

178

He jogs upstairs, almost excited. I follow, intrigued. There are no carburettors resting on top of newspapers. I can walk straight up the middle of the staircase. It feels oddly freeing to lack constraint in Jamal's house. I'm used to tiptoeing around.

At the top of the stairs he turns right instead of the usual left. I notice that even the bathroom is clean. There are no giant pieces of scrap soaking in noxious liquids in the bathtub. The tiles are white. The sink lacks its faded black oil stains down the sides.

"Have you started seeing someone?" I ask.

Jamal's standing in front of the spare room which he uses as his workshop.

"God no," he says. "I wouldn't know where to start. Come and see."

I approach the doorway and look in. This is where all the mess is hiding. Shelves full of rusty pieces of metal line the two sidewalls like a library. The back wall's window has been covered with hardboard and has tools hanging on it. In the centre of the floor space, on a purpose-built workbench, there is a large, freshly polished engine.

I walk into the room.

There are bigger, stranger parts than usual: giant springs, huge bars of steel, long bending tubes, tyres, sheets of glass, a pile of black metal slats stacked against each other.

"What am I looking at?" I ask.

"An original 1965, one hundred and seventy-two horsepower, six point two litre, eight-valve Silver Shadow. Engine, chassis, body. The whole thing. I'm getting the upholstery redone with a specialist."

I look at him, none the wiser.

"It's a vintage Rolls Royce."

"Is this the thing that was in your bathtub last time?"

"Some of it. Look at that engine. Isn't she a beaut?"

"It's definitely an engine…" I say, walking around the workbench. "Is it worth much?"

"Money? After all the overheads, not really, no. More of a passion project. When you learn about all the relationships these pieces of metal have with each other... it's hard to explain. Let's just say, the Silver Shadow is a beautiful machine."

"Silver Shadow," I say, inspecting it and trying to see something special. "Sounds like a superhero. Is this why you invited me over? I mean, I'm sorry I'm not more impressed. I'm sure it's a big deal."

"No, man," he says, still smiling, looking at the engine. "I just wanted you to see why I'm buzzing about like a bee in a flower shop. I actually wanted to see how you were doing, after last time. You know? It's been a while."

He glances at me, concern simmering beneath the robotic flicker of his eye muscles.

"Who installed your empathy programme?"

He walks out of the room grinning and shaking his head. I follow him to his bedroom. He climbs into his usual cross-legged position and relights the unlit joint in his mouth.

"So? How are things?" he asks. "Besides the bruises we're not talking about."

I think about playing it cool and trying to enjoy our friendship without thinking or talking about everything that's going on (and Jamal would let me without probing) but sorrow rushes to my eyes and throat and I have an overwhelming need to be honest with him.

"She left me," I admit, trying to breathe slowly.

Jamal forces himself to look into my eyes.

"For good?"

"I don't know. Maybe not, at first. But I think I've messed up my chances. I was stupid. I kept too much back."

"She found out about the lithium?"

"She figured it out."

"But she left you in the house?"

"For now. It was a good job she did, to be honest."

"Is she staying at her sister's?"

"No. Her mum and dad's."

"Shit."

"I know."

Jamal's knees are beginning to bounce up and down. His eyes are wide. The emotional aspect of the conversation has made his muscles rigid, but he is still answering with sound empathy.

"Just give her time," he says. "She'll let you know what she needs. You don't want to see her whilst you look like this anyway."

"Can we talk about this later?" I say. "I was doing okay for a minute there."

"Of course. What do you want to talk about?"

I stand up and look out his window, down at the patchy, overgrown lawn. Jamal, though struggling with it, is being unusually receptive and I'm uncomfortably aware that this reflects that I'm on a low ebb, and that it's clear, even to him, that I need care and attention.

"Do you believe in signs, or messages, in nature?" I ask.

He shifts his weight on his spine and furrows his brow, but he nods slightly, motioning that he will move forward with this strange subject because talking about it might be the thing that helps me.

"I believe in a guidance system," he says, "a genetic memory, I suppose. Signs and messages can be a part of it. Like black and yellow for poison, or red for danger. It can be more complicated than that, obviously."

"I mean, more like spirit guides, that kind of thing."

"Why, what have the sprites been whispering?" he asks, trying to grin.

"Nothing I can explain without sounding crazy."

"Try me."

"No. It doesn't matter."

"Seriously. I know loads about that sort of stuff."

"No, you don't."

"I do. I'm constantly reading anthropology."

"You are?"

"You know I am."

"I thought you just read car manuals and newspapers these days."

"I was reading about the difference between Neanderthals and Homo sapiens this morning. Look."

He reaches down by the bed and hands me a book with a badly designed cover and a terrible title, *Monkey See. Monkey Do. Man Imagine*. It looks like it had a print run of about fifty. There's a picture of a professor on the back dressed like a hiker who wants to die a virgin. I hand the book back to him, dismissive of its content.

"It's too hard to explain," I say. "I made friends with this blackbird. It was following me around, telling me things, warning me, guiding me… Sorry. This sounds insane. Talking about it ruins what it was."

"Not at all. I was reading a book on Palaeolithic religion before this one, about totems and rituals. It's all fresh in my head."

"If you're about to spend half an hour calling me a Neanderthal…"

"No, man," he says, leaving his joint resting in the ashtray and picking up a squat tube of metal and some wire wool, starting to scrub. "Neanderthals were atheists by nature. They weren't capable of symbolic thought. At least, not to the extent that we were."

"Isn't the whole point of atheism the choice?"

"When Homo sapiens started believing in things they couldn't see, that's when they became human. It had nothing to do with their intelligence. Well, it did, but this book argues that the modern world has misconceived what human intelligence is."

"Enlighten me."

"So, most people think intelligence is like focus, or alertness, being objective, being able to measure things quickly and accurately, all the qualities that are valued by science, but this book says that Neanderthals were more intelligent than us in this primary way."

"So why aren't they sitting here having this conversation?"

He puts down his chunk of metal and lights his joint again.

"Think about it. Discoveries come from inspiration, visions. If Homo sapiens had objective minds there would be no culture or invention, no science or technology. We'd still be living in alpha-dominated packs."

"Why no science?" I ask.

"Because first you have to invent a theory, conceive a method, put two and two together. That's not how an objective mind behaves."

"So Homo sapiens started daydreaming and inventing things."

"Exactly."

"I don't see what this has got to do with anything."

"Okay," he says, inhaling smoke deeply. "First of all there were a select few Homo sapiens who started having visions. They taught the others how to see them by pointing them out with pigments – effectively, drawing things on rocks. Back then, a picture was inconceivable to the majority of people and the seers would have to teach them all how to see it, even after they'd drawn it."

"The seer was like a shaman or a priest or something?"

"This book just calls them seers. They were the ones who could see the pictures in the first place, before they'd marked them out for the others. And once these artworks started appearing, the seers began telling stories about where these pictures were coming from. They created entire belief systems around them. Painting a picture was like catching a spirit, bringing it into the physical world."

"I still don't see where this is going."

"I'm laying groundwork, man. Chill."

"Fine."

"Okay, so the interesting thing, the relevant thing, is that one of the most recurring things we hear about these seers, from deepest Africa to Western Europe, is that – without any contact or communication between tribes – they consistently documented the fact that they had spirit animals, usually birds, protecting them and guiding them to the truth."

"Birds?"

"A spirit animal was considered a badge of honour, given directly to the seer by the great spirit of nature. In those days it was the equivalent of having a well-funded research laboratory. If you had recurring visions of a spirit animal, or if a certain kind of wild animal was consistently tame in your presence, then your theories and inspirations were believed to be nature's sacred truths."

"Basically, you're saying that forty thousand years ago society would have deemed me an important person but now I'm just a whack job who should have studied science."

Jamal laughs smoke out through his nose and stubs out the end of his joint.

"People who experienced periods where they couldn't see reality were revered as sacred and wise."

"You are. You're saying my brain has been stuck in some kind of retrogressive caveman state."

"No. You're not getting it. The Homo sapiens' ability to imagine and interpret complex imagery, to make contact with meaning and project it onto the world, that was what marked their heightened intelligence. That was how they evolved beyond the animals."

"So imagination is a kind of intelligence?"

"The human kind. Basically, when a seer conceived of his totem, that was the sign he was becoming more intelligent, figuring something out. It meant that the two sides of his consciousness had started communicating with each other. His tribe would put up with all sorts of shit from him because when he came back to reality he always brought something with him: knowledge, stories, ideas."

He starts to build another joint.

"But you're also saying that all those seers were crazy."

"No. I'm saying that, in the first instance, insight is subjective."

"Still, you're saying that all the spiritualism was imaginary. None of these seers ever truly had a spirit animal."

"The seers didn't know how to differentiate between good and bad visions, true and false ones. Psychosis, creativity, it was all just supernatural and mystical and therefore true. But the codes and laws they formed over time, the things we kept hold of – science, law, narrative, art, ritual – these are the things that make us human, what makes society worthwhile."

"But you said these seers, thousands of miles apart, all claimed to have spirit animals. Maybe that's what happens when people connect to a deeper facet of nature. We just forgot how to do it."

"It's more likely that spirit animals were the first severance from nature, the beginning of culture."

"When it was happening, I knew it wasn't real, I knew it could never be measured, but, equally, it was just as convincing as reality. There was something incomprehensible all around me, nothing to do with time or space. The blackbirds, Charlie, they were just the signs it chose to guide me."

Jamal, about to lick the gum on his new joint, stops and looks up.

"Charlie?"

"I saw Charlie. A few times."

"Shit, man."

"I know it wasn't him. Not really. But I don't think it was me either."

He seals his joint, prods it with a match and lights it.

"I can't help seeing it the way I do," he says. "Take the engine across the hall, when I get it running it'll sound like it's got a life of its own, the power it creates will seem like it's coming from nowhere but it comes from the fact that it's part of a system, gathered over the years, slowly getting more and more complex, until lots of knowledge is crammed into a tiny space. It might not look like it's got anything in common with a rowing boat's oars but it does. The collective power of all the previous engines is carried forward within it. It's the same with the unconscious mind. There's some inherent knowledge passed down from our ancestors, more than just instincts, something that can help us understand what's true, how to move forward, how to deal with life. We project it onto the world around us because that's the way our brains work. That's how we find meaning."

"But why are you so sure? Why can't you accept reality as an incomplete idea, something we can never fully grasp? There's no telling what's in here with us, what sends us meaning, what lies beyond us, what can't be measured or understood. We have to accept the uncertainty of it all."

"I guess that's why you're the writer and I'm the mechanic."

"Maybe," I say, standing up and walking towards the door.

"Where are you going?" he asks. "I've not annoyed you, have I?"

"No. Everything you've said makes complete sense."

"What's wrong then?"

"It just... it makes *too much* sense."

"What does?"

"Sorry, I've got to go."

"Why?"

"I've just realised what's going to happen in my book."

I leave the room.

"Your book?"

"*On the great map of the spirit only a few points are illuminated*," I call back.

"But you haven't even told me where you got your bruises."

"Another time," I shout, from the stairs. "I've got to go."

TWO

There are four fundamental forces in nature. Quantum mechanics' probabilistic theories led to the comprehension of three: the strong nuclear force, the electromagnetic force and the weak nuclear force. Gravity was understood slightly earlier, using the classical rules of general relativity. However, since the micro quantum-universe is mathematically incompatible with the macro classical-universe, a singular framework that incorporates all four fundamental forces has not yet been discovered. Physicists know what the forces are and what they do. They know how to measure and predict their behaviours. They just can't prove that they exist in the same universe.

I've spent the last month in a very different kind of isolation, writing and editing as much as ten hours a day; lonely but focused and productive. My novel has been finished and redrafted many times over but I keep reading and reading it, just to make sure. The first read-through took over twelve hours but now I'm so familiar with the material I can get through it in four. I'm at the point where there's nothing else I can do without somebody else's opinion.

The end has come at a good time. Today's going to be the first chance I've had to see Lyd since she walked out of the anomaly scan whilst I was heaving over a bin. I go out for a run in the hope of vitalising myself, so I don't seem like somebody bound to a desk, starved of human contact. I avoid Hampstead Heath because I'm not quite ready to re-enter that strange land where I lost myself. My psyche is still slightly raw and my body has only just healed. Instead, I do a couple of slow laps around the much smaller Waterlow Park and then walk over into Highgate Cemetery.

This is the cemetery where Charlie is buried. We were lucky to get him in here, apparently. They only accept thirty new bodies a year. His grave is small and discreet. I have no idea how much it cost but it must have been expensive. I don't even know who paid for it.

I stop, like always, at George Eliot's small cenotaph. I take a moment to think about her writing, her insight and empathy, her commitment to realism. She was always one of my greatest inspirations and, at a formative age, gave me the first sensations of psychological transcendence that made me want to become a writer. Her work is like a friend that I'm always glad is inside me and her grave always calms me before I move on to see Charlie's.

Walking on, I recall my obsession with Charlie's decomposition. For months, rolling around in bed, I would find myself imagining the state of his dead body in its coffin. Again and again I wished he'd been cremated but I was too scared to share this with Lyd. Not only because I had been too manic and too far gone to attend the funeral (or even conceive of it) but because I didn't want to bring a new and unimagined kind of torment down on her. There was a chance that she hadn't even thought of his body rotting and decaying in its coffin.

When I see his grave I'm glad that he's buried. Cremation tiles, all bundled together, are less personal. The dead become a brick in a wall. There's no space for memories to breathe. Here I can pull away weeds, tend to old flowers and keep his little garden under control. The bones beneath are proof that he truly existed – an anchor: invisible, but adding weight and stillness to my memories.

The grave also adds a sense of settlement to my life in London. Highgate once seemed like an alienating suburb that I shouldn't be able to afford to live in, part of a city too big to call home. Now, this tiny plot of land makes me feel like I really belong here, because someone I truly loved is buried in its earth.

I realise that this is the first time I've stood at Charlie's graveside and felt like he's really dead. I don't sense his essence lurking or shining in the world around me. The feeling of his being, my collected memory of him, comes from the inside instead of outside. I still long for him but the longing is distant, less brutal.

At home I shower and shave and then pick up fresh fruit and vegetables for a healthy lunch. I feel prepared, ready to face life head on. Rather than pick me up, I've arranged to meet Lyd at the NHS antenatal services centre because I don't want her to feel like she has to drive me around, or that I rely on her to do practical things.

I arrive early and wait outside. The NHS building was once an affluent Georgian home, probably converted in the early fifties. There's space to park eight cars in what was once a front garden. Being on a residential street, it looks slightly out of place but there's also a dentist's office, a solicitor's office and two nursing homes.

Lyd arrives in a taxi looking tired. I can't believe how bulbous she is. She's walking on her heels like an obese person. She hardly says a word to me when I greet her. We walk into the building with our heads bowed; lone agents of parenthood. I have an image of a room bathed in soft white light, with modern furnishings and laminate floors, where a circle of loving couples sit toboggan-style, four hands on every bump, forging lifelong friendships whilst me and Lyd sit side by side struggling with our proximity.

The clinic is all beige and pale greens. There are pin boards, health posters, tables of flyers, acrylic signs, plastic chairs, dozens of health-and-safety notices and laminated notifications from the staff who are trying to make their own jobs easier. The round wooden reception island exhibits a level of carpentry and quality of wood that suggests it predates the cheap eighties' refit. Old kinds of death and suffering seep through its cracks and scratches.

Lyd speaks to the receptionist and we're directed to a classroom. The whole building is austere and downtrodden. Parts of the corridor are barely even lit. It's a long way from the bright twenty-first-century pillar of technology where we went for our ultrasounds but it's the only place we could find that would take us on such short notice (our communications and arrangements regarding the pregnancy had fallen by the wayside over the last few months).

The set-up of the room and the people populating it are nothing like my projected image. Twenty tired couples sit in uniform rows on cheap plastic chairs barely speaking to each other. The room is what I imagine night school looks like, but with lots more posters of babies and no desks. Me and Lyd approach the second row to take the last two chairs, causing a calamitous recession of pregnant bellies and awkward men as we make our way past.

The room, with over forty people in it, is eerily quiet. Blue light bouncing off the projector screen seems to have drawn everybody into a hypnotic state of submission. We all wait for a stout, depressed-looking midwife to connect wires and fiddle with a laptop.

Eventually, an image is projected. It has a white, baby blue and soft yellow colour scheme and is brimming with bad clip art. The stout midwife closes the blinds, turns off the electric lights and proceeds to spout over an hour of obvious, common sense information whilst clicking a little button and making exactly what she's saying appear on the screen behind her. It is the epitome of a bad presentation.

At the hour mark I look at Lyd and see that she is loathing the dull woman at the front as much as I am.

"Want to go?" I ask her in a whisper.

She looks at me like I just spat on our unborn baby and did I not know that the important bit was coming up in just a minute?

When the presentation finally comes to an end, after each of the seven subheadings has had its bland ten minutes (1: Health, 2: Exercise, 3: Labour and Birth, 4: Pain and Relaxation, 5: Care, 6: Emotions and 7: Health – again!), the midwife turns the lights back on and, in a monotone, announces:

"Okay, everybody stand up and move your chairs to the sides of the room. We're going to swap partners and try a little role play."

Lyd's shoulders slump and hang low. She looks at me with adolescent reluctance.

"Fine," she says. "Let's get out of here."

I jump to my feet and hold my hand out behind me before she changes her mind. She grabs it and I lead her through a corridor of knees, distended wombs, shoes and thin metal chair legs. As we reach the door the midwife's dreary voice calls after us:

"Shyer couples can sit this one out if they prefer."

We both look back at her and shake our heads with feigned amusement and ambiguity, trying to imply that something else is pulling us away from this interesting and essential class.

Once we are out in the corridor we both sigh with relief and smile at each other. Realising we're holding hands our smiles become awkward so we let go and begin walking towards the exit.

"Why do the extroverts who script these things always assume that introverts are broken versions of themselves who just need a little bit of repression workshopped out of them?" asks Lyd.

"Probably the same reason we think they're self-indulgent idiots who need a little bit of self-reflection and doubt forced into them."

"I know it's just a team-building exercise, making everybody feel like they're in it together so they can break down barriers and make friends, but I really can't abide it when things are that psychologically transparent. It's embarrassing. Anyone with any intelligence feels forced to respond ironically or knowingly and then they find themselves trapped in a rebellion that's even more pathetic than engaging with the process."

"And then all the rebels have to try to mockingly justify their appeasement to the process when they inevitably join in."

"Whilst the more self-pitying of them wonder why they can never find a comfortable role in a group."

"And the more confident of them ponder why everybody appropriates a psychological type whenever a group forms and thinks they're so clever to keep their strong individual self so hidden but so present."

"And the rest of the group are thinking, we all know that this exercise is stupid. You lot are just the maladjusted idiots who want lots of attention because you didn't get any love in your childhoods."

"But really we deserve all the attention because we were well-behaved children and that's why Mummy and Daddy stayed together and loved us."

"I hate it," she says, smiling.

"Me too."

We've just left the building but our conversation feels so natural and amusing that we carry on walking together. At the end of the street we turn left and go into the first coffee shop we see without even acknowledging that we've made a decision to stay together. This excites me and there's a tiny sparkle in Lyd's eyes that reflects the same.

"Maybe we are a bit too anti-social," I say, as we stand in the queue.

"Undoubtedly. But that doesn't affect the world in any negative way. There's no reason to surround ourselves with people if we don't enjoy it."

"We're just not built for groups."

"Some people are more useful on the peripheries."

"Exactly," I say. "And we do okay. We're good in smaller, more tight-knit groups."

"Sometimes," says Lyd. "Personally, I think we both thrive when we're alone. I've got so much more work done since I've been at Mum and Dad's."

"Me too actually," I admit, reluctantly.

At the counter, even though I'm desperately poor and thinking that today might be a good opportunity to bring up the fact that I can't afford the electricity bill (the only bill in my name), I make a point of buying the drinks: black coffee for me and peppermint tea for Lyd.

We sit at a small table by the window. Now that we're facing each other the easy mood has become more difficult. There is a long silence. Lyd's expression is serious and solemn. I fiddle with a sugar packet until I notice her scrutinising my twiddling fingers.

"I'm sorry," I start. "I should have handled things better."

"Please, don't launch into a big thing."

"But we need to talk."

"Shall I sum up what you're about to say and save us both a couple of hours?" she says. I shrug, half prompting her. "Okay. It goes like this – I was wrong. But I was also right. I'm sorry I was right. But I was right. I'm really sorry being right upset you. You were right too. And no less right than me. In some ways, everybody's always right. Isn't life confusing? Have you forgiven me yet?"

"Be fair."

"That's your standard apology."

"I hate it when you do that."

"What?"

"Mock me for trying to be honest."

"You always want to talk but it doesn't change anything."

"I think it helps, even if you just sit there parodying me. It's getting something out there."

"It doesn't help me."

"We've barely spoken for months."

"We didn't need to. We needed time... You know, I thought we might be able to have one drink where we weren't weighed down by things we need to get through. You know? Something light."

"I'm sorry. I want that too."

She looks away from me, out the window.

"Too late," she says.

"I guess..."

"I don't think we can be good parents. We're too messed up, too self-involved."

"So? I hate good parents. Good parents make me want to kick children in the face."

She smirks.

"I think we might function better apart."

"No."

"I'm afraid that I might not love you anymore."

She looks at me for a moment, and then down at the table. Her hand passes over her stomach and she frowns.

"When it kicks it always feels so far away."

"Come home with me, Lyd."

"I'm not coming home."

"We can make it right together."

"No. We can't."

"I don't understand."

"Don't pull that face. I'm just being honest."

"At least come back to the house. I can sleep on the couch, stay at Jamal's; whatever you need. Surely your parents give you less space than I could?"

"I still need time away from the house."

She puts both hands on her stomach now. There is a note of melancholy in her eyes, as though her hands are ears that hear nothing.

"If you need time, you need time," I say.

"I do."

"What are we facing here? Do you think we'll ever be together again?"

"I'm sorry, Vince. I can't answer that."

"Why not?"

"Because the answer is no…"

She looks at me apologetically.

"I'm hoping the answer is going to change," she says.

"But I'm out of the woods. I'm better. I've been working, focused. My book's finished…"

At the mention of my writing Lyd looks at her watch.

"I better get back. Peter's coming to pick me up."

"No. Wait. Can we talk more? I want to spend time with you. We can make it light."

"No, we can't, Vince. That's the problem… I've got to go."

"Why is Peter picking you up?"

"He's going to take me back to Mum and Dad's, have a meal with us. I got the train this morning."

"Let me walk you to the car."

"No. You don't have to. You're closer to home here."

"I want to."

"Fine. You can walk me to my brother's car."

We leave the coffee shop.

Lyd wraps her elbow around mine, cautiously, as though testing for feelings. At one point she rests her temple on my shoulder and grabs my arm with her other hand – still placid, still wondering. My left side fizzes with nervous pleasure. My manner becomes more stiff and cautious because I'm trying to avoid the inevitable moment when I say the wrong thing or act the wrong way and lose her fragile affections. This anxiety is immediately intuited by Lyd and she lets go, walking with her eyes fixedly ahead. The last thirty metres was a tactile indulgence that we are now supposed to pretend didn't happen.

Peter is already waiting in the antenatal centre's small car park, sitting in his two-seater Audi. He gets out of his car when he sees us.

"They all came out five minutes ago."

"Sorry," says Lyd.

"Hi, Peter."

He nods at me, half able to reveal his contempt for my existence now that he thinks his sister might be leaving me.

"Where've you been?" he asks.

"We went for a hot drink," says Lyd. "It was horrible in there."

"We should get going or we'll hit the traffic on the way out."

"I forgot to book my appointment with the midwife. Sorry. I won't be a minute."

Lyd walks back towards the entrance. I'm left standing with Peter. He sniffs every couple of seconds. The comedowns from the cocaine and benzodiazepines are beginning to make his eyes sink and withdraw. He's not too far away from the point where I'll have to object to Lyd getting in a car with him. For now he's a highly functioning addict but he's definitely treading the border between overconfidence and self-annihilation.

"What happened with you and Gloria in the end?" I ask him.

(I know that it didn't work out but I can't help myself.)

"*Gloria*?" he says, mockingly. "I haven't thought about her in months."

"No?"

"On to pastures new."

"You seemed pretty set on her last time I saw you."

A flicker of hatred crosses his eyes. He wants to destroy me for having seen him in a state of weakness. He needs everybody to believe that he is strong.

"I should have known better than to get involved with any of your people," he says.

"My people?"

"She'd rather scream at a gambling addict than have something good in her life."

"I hear coke-heads make much better partners."

"You don't know anything about me."

"I know adultery isn't the best foundation for a relationship," I say, "especially with your sister's friend... I'm sorry you got hurt though."

"She did me a favour."

"Why's that?"

"She reminded me how duplicitous women truly are."

I turn away from him with a smile of disbelief.

"You should be grateful you felt something," I say. "I didn't even know you had feelings."

"You talk like a teenage girl. It annoys me that you can even annoy me. If it wasn't for..."

"What?"

He squares up to me and glances at the entrance to the building.

"You know, don't you? That you don't deserve Lydia?"

He takes a breath, leaning back, and claps his hands in front of my face. I try but don't wholly manage to restrain a flinch.

"She always went for the fuck-ups," he continues, pivoting away from me. "You just happened to be the fuck-up who got her pregnant."

"You have no idea what me and Lyd have been through," I say, my spine trembling slightly, my bladder tightening.

He steps back towards me.

"We're not talking about Charlie here, Vince. Don't hide behind that. We're talking about you being a waste of space. Why don't you just piss off out of that house and leave her to get on with her life?"

His expression is desolate. My heart is beating fast. There are no words in my head. I feel inferior, undeserving of his sister's love.

Lyd reappears in the doorway.

Peter finds instant resolve and smiles for her. I take a deep breath. For the first time, I see a kind of moral strength and integrity in Peter. He might be a sociopath, but he also loves his sister.

"You two look very serious," she says.

"We've just been having a chat," says Peter.

"I hope it wasn't about me?"

"It wasn't about you," I say.

"We were talking about his future."

Lyd shrugs her shoulders.

"I think you two are really starting to get to grips with each other, aren't you?"

I smile at her.

"Come on," says Peter. "Let's beat that traffic."

THREE

People used to believe that the gateway to the Otherworld opened for a short while at the end of the harvest season, allowing all the dead souls to pass through. Places were set at tables and food was offered to dead ancestors out of respect and remembrance. Fare was also left outside to keep darker spirits' mischief and trickery at bay. These ritual offerings gradually became the sweets and chocolates that home owners gave to wandering children dressed as the dead, who, on their reception, announced the option, 'Trick or treat?' By this point in time the gateway to the Otherworld had been long presumed closed. Darkness was just empty space. The dead were just dead.

I had to do a lot of preparation to end up looking like Frankenstein's monster. I have bolts stuck on my neck, grey-green skin, a tattered black jumper and overcoat, black trousers and big black boots. The real work went into adding the latex cap that adds two inches to my forehead and gives me that deformed, receding monster look.

I already had this outfit. Lyd has the Bride of Frankenstein wig with the two white zigzag stripes up the sides. She wears it with a long white nightgown, white face make-up, dark eyes and bandages all up her arms. We've been to three Halloween parties together dressed this way and it always seems clear, even when we're standing apart, that we're together. Lyd won't be wearing her Bride of Frankenstein outfit tonight. It's still in the box at home.

Gloria and Sergio's house is decorated with fake spiderwebs, expertly cut pumpkins and plastic insects and ghouls. The lights are low. In the front room there's a projection of a ghost that loiters on the living room wall. Every five minutes or so, it turns into a giant skull with a wide open jaw and a loud scream rips through the room. All the songs are themed. So far we've had "Monster Mash", "I Was a Teenage Werewolf" and "Ghostbusters". The house is full of people in fancy dress. I don't know any of them.

Sergio's friends are all corporate lawyers and efficiency experts, and other jobs that require a psychopathic streak (or, like Sergio, a series of mini – and early – midlife crises). They have mostly come as famous murderers. There's a lazy guy who's just hung a plastic chainsaw around his neck and put it over the top of his work suit – a Patrick Bateman cop out (yet uncomfortably convincing). Freddy Krueger, Myra Hindley, Leatherface and a man in a miscellaneous orange jumpsuit are all seemingly talking about their favourite kill and laughing.

Despite Gloria's profession being similar her friends are a broader mix of people: some university friends, people from an old workplace, others from leisure activities and a few select people from her current job. There's a tendency toward the sexy in the women – cats, witches and rabbits in tiny skirts and fishnets – and lots of zombies and a couple of vampires amongst the men.

The only two I can't work out are a couple who have come as Magenta and Riff Raff from *The Rocky Horror Picture Show*. Sexy and psycho, they must be mutual friends of them both.

I can't see Lyd anywhere.

I'm on my second pumpkin punch (which is surprisingly good – I get the feeling professionals might have done the decorating and put on the spread). It's served in a white plastic cup in the shape of a skull. Sergio, dressed as Gomez Addams, sees me standing alone and heads towards me.

Gloria is dressed as Morticia. They are extremely well-suited to their roles, which are extremely well-suited to hosting a Halloween party at home, so they are both fairly proud of how they look.

"I hate your friends," I say.

"Me too. Me too," says Sergio, looking around.

"Who *are* they?"

"They're not all completely evil," he says. "I met Freddy Krueger over there at my gambling group. He's a sweet, sweet man. He's been through hell."

"How come all your buddies came as serial killers?"

"It's Halloween."

"I've been *psycho*analysing the costumes."

"I'm sure you have. Me too actually. Don't you think zombies are very working man? You know, powerless sheep stumbling through life until the next payday."

"The zombies are the only ones I want to talk to."

"That's because you're attracted to depression."

"You talk such rubbish. Did you invite Jamal?"

"Every year."

"Has he ever come?"

"Nope."

"Any sign of Lyd?"

"About that," he says. "I wanted to tell you in person... I'm sorry I wasn't there for you when—"

"We've been through this."

"I know but I feel like—"

"I told you not to worry about it. You had your own thing going on."

"I know but... anyway... I don't think she's here yet."

"How are things on the home front?"

"Are you asking or are you being polite?"

"I'm asking."

"Fucking tough. I messed up big this time."

"She messed up too though."

"You only know half of it."

"Do I want to know?"

"Let's just say the roulette wheel took a couple of Porsches out the bank on either side of Mitsu. And staying in hotels for three months wasn't cheap either."

"Shit."

"She screwed around. I screwed around. Lust is a tricky bastard. Everyone knows that. When things get rough it's easy to mess things up that way. The gambling though. That's separate. I promised her I'd never do that to us again. The trust is gone."

"Totally gone?"

"Not like when I lost the house, but bad."

"What happened to Mitsu?"

"The less you know about Mitsu the better."

"Fair enough. Does Lyd know that it was Peter yet?"

Sergio grimaces.

"Yeah. She's had it out with Gloria already. You wouldn't know to look at them. Hey, hey, hey, look who it is."

I turn my head. Gloria is walking Lyd through to the kitchen. Lyd is wearing a nineteenth-century gothic black dress with test tubes in a utility belt. It has long sleeves and a high neck. Her bump looks huge in it. Leatherface and Patrick Bateman leer over Gloria's cleavage as they pass.

"I shouldn't have come as Frankenstein's monster," I say. "I should have come as Venkman or something. I don't want her to see me like this."

"Frankenstein's your thing," says Sergio. "It's literary."

"No. It's *our* thing. She's supposed to be the Bride, remember? It's cinematic. Halloweeny. I'm going to have to change. Have you got a white sheet or something?"

"Vince, take a breath. She wouldn't have come if she didn't want to talk to you. I thought things were getting better? You were making progress?"

"What does she expect me to say? Last time I saw her she said all this weird stuff about us being better off alone. Since

202

then we've just been talking rubbish on the phone, trying to prove I can make things feel light again."

"As far as I'm concerned, her coming all this way can only be a good sign. This could be the first night you get to take her home again."

"You think?"

"Definitely. Why else would she travel fifty odd miles or whatever it is to come to some lame Halloween party? You think she wants to stay in Peckham with her sister when yours is just down the road?"

"I'm so embarrassed. I should have got a new costume."

He takes me by the shoulders.

"Vince. Forget about the costume. She doesn't care about the costume. She's pregnant with your child."

"You're right. You're right."

"Take a deep breath and down the rest of that punch."

I do what he says.

"Now, go get her."

"If this goes wrong I'm going to be Cousin It next year, living in your basement."

"That's it. Summon up some of that famous Watergate positivity."

He slaps me on the back as I walk towards the kitchen. Seeing me approach, Gloria stops talking and fixes her eyes on me until Lyd turns her head. They stare at me with bad smells in their noses.

When I get to where they're standing, before I speak, Gloria rests her hand on Lyd's shoulder sympathetically. Lyd turns to her, forces a smile and nods. Gloria gives her shoulder a little squeeze and walks by me with a blank face.

"Who are you?" I ask. "I mean, what's your costume?"

"Marie Curie," she says.

I shrug.

"The first woman to win a Nobel prize?"

"Sorry," I say, apologising for my ignorance.

I look at her large bump sticking out, our child.

"I see you're the monster again…"

I smile awkwardly. Lyd replies with a twitch of her right cheek. It's supposed to be a polite flash of a smile but it doesn't make an impression on her lips.

"So," she says, almost a question.

"Lame party."

"Yep."

Riff Raff and Magenta have come into the kitchen and are showing off their creepy sibling lovers' handshake to a pirate and a vampire. I watch them and wonder what to say. Lyd runs her right hand across her stomach. Magenta is beginning to perform the opening dialogue to the "Time Warp". Riff Raff joins in. I have to look away.

"How's work?" I ask.

"There's never a dull moment below the Planck length."

"The plank what?"

"Never mind."

My mobile phone vibrates in my pocket. Quickly glancing at the screen I see that it's my mum calling. I think about all the possible inanities that I could ignore but none of them cover this time on Halloween night. I walk a couple of steps away and answer.

"Hi, Mum. Everything okay?"

"Hi, love. I don't know how to say this. Are you at home?"

"I'm at a Halloween party. Say what?"

"It's your dad."

"My *dad*?"

"Yes," she says.

"What about him?"

"The hospice rang. He only has a few days left… He wants to see you."

"He wants to see me?"

"He's dying. Cancer."

"He's dying and he wants to see me?"

"That's what they said."

"Why?"

"You're his son, Vince."

"I know that."

"That's all they said. He wants to see you."

"I don't know about this."

"You might regret it if you don't go."

"I might regret it if I do."

"You can stay with us, if you come. John will drive you up there if Lyd's not... well, you won't tell me anything about what's going on. If she doesn't, if she's not—"

"I need to think about this."

"You don't have time to think about it. You either come or you don't. He's on his last legs."

"Okay," I say. "I'll ring you in the morning and let you know."

"Remember he's your dad, Vince. Whether he was a good one or not, he's still your dad."

"I know, Mum. I've got to go."

Being dressed like Frankenstein's monster suddenly seems ridiculous, as does dressing up in general. The whole party is surreal and absurd. I need to leave but my first instinct is to tell Lyd about the phone call. She is my barometer of truth. By talking to her I'll know how I feel. It also occurs to me that this is a serious thing, an important moment, and, as such, if I'm still important to her, I'll be able to see in her response where we stand.

I turn back to her.

"My mum," I say, waggling my phone before I put it back in my pocket. "Apparently, well, my dad's dying."

"Your *dad*?"

"Cancer. He wants to see me."

"He wants to *see* you?"

"So she says."

"Are you going to go?"

"I don't know."

"Do you want to?"

"I guess. More for curiosity than anything."

Lyd is fully immersed in my situation, sympathetic, but she catches herself at it. She forces her emotional tides to recede, moving heaven and earth so that she can seem resolved in her decision not to share the burden of my problems. I see this struggle in her face and find it hard to blame her, especially after seeing that her instinct was to come forward, towards me. Her reticence is born of trauma and pain. Her hand wanders over her pregnant stomach again.

"Sorry you have to go through this," she says, deadpan now, rational. "It's bad timing."

"I'm not sure I'm going through anything," I say. "I can't go anyway."

"What do you mean *can't* go?"

"I don't want to talk about it."

"Tell me."

"I can't."

"Tell me."

I stare at a plastic bat hanging from a light fitting. Beneath my green make-up my cheeks are burning. I'm glad that some portion of my embarrassment is covered but I know that Lyd will be able to see it in my eyes.

"Well?" she says.

"I can't afford the train ticket."

"Are you kidding me?"

"I can barely afford food."

"You're a child, Vince, a *child*."

"I know."

She shakes her head with an exasperated grin.

"Fine."

"What?" I ask.

"I'll take you."

"You'll take me?"

"Yes, I'll take you. If you want to go?"

"I think so," I say, grabbing the opportunity to be with her for an extended period. "I mean, I do."

"You're hopeless. You know that, don't you?"

I nod but, beneath my shame, beneath my dying father, beneath my overdraft limit, there is a tiny glimmer. She could have just offered me the money for the train ticket but instead she's coming with me.

FOUR

The objective truth is a concept formed within subjective realities about a wider reality. Words and numbers are constantly added to this extremely complicated concept, expanding its sign system. When its underlying rules are wholly understood and the objective truth has been fully expressed, further signs and significations will only ever enhance and readdress what is already known. Having come of age, the objective truth will be celebrated and made available to everybody. People will analyse more or less of it, tell stories about it, make discoveries with it, progress or regress because of it, believe in it or dismiss it, but, most importantly, they will remain separate from it.

London recedes like a sea we've been swimming in. We drive past inert industrial zones, warehouses, piles of stones and sand, silos and long chutes. Monolithic chunks of concrete fly backwards, glass flashes, wires bounce, brick walls smear into clay smudges. Dirt and soot taints the first fields but the colours gradually become more vibrant and natural. Birds begin to outnumber aeroplanes. There are more orange and red tree roofs than grey and terracotta house roofs.

My MP3 player is plugged into the car stereo, set on random. "Venus in Furs" by the Velvet Underground begins to play. Fixing my eyes on the middle distance, the fast-moving tarmac and traffic seems almost stationary. John

Cale's discordant viola and Lou Reed's wooing voice send me into a reverie about when I first met Lyd.

A large group of us were out in Victoria Park for Bonfire Night. She was a friend of a friend of a friend, just starting out as a particle physicist, obsessed with M-theory and mini-black holes and unable to talk about anything else. I found her passion fresh and exciting. Unlike me, talking with self-interest about the novel I was working on, her work sounded important, it was new ground, it was adding to how people would understand the universe in the years to come. She made me appreciate how selfless and meaningful the pursuit of science was.

I remember watching her face as light from the fireworks glowed on her skin. Her expression did not contain the same vacant joy of the others. It was philosophical, but not pretentious. She was bathing in the chemistry of gunpowder, the physics of light and sound, space and time. She was as infatuated with the mysteries of science as I was with her.

At the end of the night we exchanged numbers, promised each other coffee and soon found ourselves in constant contact, sharing stories and spending all our free time together. I couldn't believe she wanted to know me. I felt so lucky.

"What are you thinking about?" asks Lyd.

Another song is playing now, something by Credence Clearwater Revival. I can't remember the title. The vocal is full of passion and honesty and the rhythm guitar is chugging and rolling. The tarmac passes quickly beneath the car. I'm full of sad love for Lyd.

"I don't know," I say. "Nothing really."

"Your dad?"

"No. Not him."

We sit in silence for a while. I watch her driving from the corner of my eye and take a moment to imagine the position of the baby inside her bump.

"Do you ever think about death?" she asks.

"Sure. All the time."

"No, I mean, what it actually is."

"I wonder whether it's an actual force of nature, something inside time that makes things deteriorate and die, or if it's more like an abstract drive in our minds and all the physical stuff is just part of the nature of systems."

"No. I'm talking about the afterlife, nothingness, that kind of thing."

"Do you, think about it?"

"Sometimes. Since. You know."

"When I was a kid, from when I was about five until I was eight, I became obsessed with this idea that when you died you met God and he showed you every single thing that was ever said or thought about you. So it didn't matter what people said or thought about you now because you'd find out everything when you were dead."

"That's cute," she says, with a smile. "And an ingenious way of beating your socially obsessive streak at its own game."

"I don't really believe in identity after death though," I say. "Not really. A mind and a memory are part of a brain and a body. Even if I could stretch myself to believe in some kind of energy transference, or a bigger life force, it wouldn't make much difference to what a person became when they were dead. Why do you ask?"

"I had this weird dream that made me start questioning a few things."

"What things?"

"It was one of those big dreams. You know, the kind that seem as important as real experiences, when they change something inside you. It was based on the idea that what you do in life is what you're stuck with after you're gone."

"Go on."

Lyd tenses her arms, grips the steering wheel tight, takes a breath and loosens up again.

"So in this dream, I'm dead, and I know I'm dead, and I'm in this empty blackness, like outer space. There are no stars or planets or anything like that. It's just this endless nothing, but I also know that it's where all the dead souls go. Nothing happens for ages, aeons. It's really boring. But I'm slowly understanding that I haven't retained my human form. Instead, everything I ever said, everything I ever did or thought has been transformed into this bizarre spirit sign. I'm like a ghost but also a signpost – it's me, every single aspect of me, transformed into the language of the dead. I never get to see my own spirit sign, I just know that that's what I am now. Eventually, I start bumping into other dead souls. And they're completely exposed before me, as I am to them. One glance is everything, all at once. All their strengths and weaknesses, all the moments they're ashamed of, all the right and wrong, how they felt and behaved, what they regretted, who they were, who they wanted to be. And all this is signified with strange emblems and foreign markings, wood, eyeballs, gemstones, feathers; all kinds of crazy stuff. I couldn't communicate with the other dead souls because everything I could ever say was said during this one second of exposure. I didn't have a mouth anymore anyway. The frequency of bumping into the dead souls was varied. The dream seemed to go on for months. Sometimes it was like rush hour in Holborn but other times I spent days in the black before I bumped into anyone. Pointless, eternal, in death you became everything you ever were in life, forever."

I laugh.

"That's pretty messed up. And, for you, very moralistic."

"But it was relative moralism. The morals of the person were part of the context of the spirit sign: they gave insight into their behaviours. It really made me think about how I'm choosing to live my life."

"And did you feel the need for any major changes?"

"I'm not sure. The thing was, I bumped into your dead soul."

"My dead soul?"

"Uh-huh."

"And?"

"And it was beautiful. I really liked it. We just kept looking at each other and even though there were all these new dark bits and these weird bits we didn't know about, it just felt right."

"I wish I could have a look at your dead soul."

"Well, I've seen yours."

"And then what?"

"Then I woke up."

The implications behind telling me about this dream might suggest she feels like she has treated me too harshly, that we only have so much time on this planet and we should be spending it together, but hopelessness stops me from responding as though this is the context of the story. Lyd has not been directing any love my way.

"Let's just hope death is the end of it," I say.

"I think it probably is."

"Me too."

We both look ahead.

The hypnosis of the motorway pulls us back in. The cities we edge around become smaller the further north we go. After the Northern Belt, cities give way to towns, towns to villages, villages to farms. When farms give way to reserves there is suddenly more nature than civilisation. Particularly after Lancaster, the views of the Lake District and the North Pennines on either side of the car keep us quiet and satisfied. I feel like London has made me forget what the planet is made of. And here it is: the greater truth.

As we pass through Eden Valley there is an enormous cloud of starlings in a murmuration, whipping and bulging in perfect synchrony above a wood of red and orange trees. The sky is a crystalline dark blue with diamond stars beginning to glow. There must be a hundred thousand starlings, many of them recent migrants, here for England's mild Gulf Stream winter. Their flight patterns resemble the movements of magnetised metal but there is no giant magnet being waved around, no conductor. They fly freely, each with their own individual will, and collectively, definitively part of their cloud.

"You know, I read somewhere—"

"Here we go. Vince read somewhere. Probably the Internet but let's pretend it was the National Archive."

"Okay, okay," I say, smiling.

"Sorry. Go on."

"In the 1890s this guy, Eugene somebody, he was obsessed with taking all the birds mentioned in Shakespeare's plays over to America. Anyway, he released one hundred starlings in Central Park. Most of the species he took over there didn't survive but by the 1990s there were two hundred million starlings in North America."

"I think the same thing happened with blackbirds in New Zealand."

I try to ignore this.

"The strange thing is, in the same period, clouds of starlings disappeared from London altogether. There used to be thousands living underneath London Bridge. There were once so many of them perching on Big Ben's minute hand that the clock came to a standstill. Now there's hardly any. There hasn't been a cloud of starlings above London in decades."

"If I was a bird I don't think I'd live in London."

"Probably not. But I wonder what the breaking point was. How did they all decide to move away?"

"Things only live where they can survive."

I nod.

We've been on the road for over four hours. The sky is darkening. The roads are narrowing. Hedgerows and ditches replace grass verges. There are no lamp posts and, a little further along, no cat's eyes. Trees obscure the sky. Twigs scratch at the doors. The speed of the car's movement is beginning to feel dangerous. The way ahead is full of blind corners and potential collisions. When the road dips our headlights illuminate less than a metre in front of us. The blackness is immediate, and infinitely dense.

We pull up to my childhood home (in a village outside Carlisle) and drop our bags off. On the doorstep my mum enacts an overly sympathetic sadness even though there is a smaller and more honest sadness behind her eyes. My stepdad, John, shows solidarity by standing up, away from his laptop, next to Mum. Chelsea lurks by them too, kindly keeping her mobile phone in her pocket (though the tips of her left-hand fingers are passing over the bulge to make sure that it's still there).

It occurs to me that they are making this man's death about me even though I barely knew him. I'm not sure if I'm supposed to say something meaningful or make a throwaway statement to ease them out of their sympathy. Maybe I'm supposed to have a feeling and express it. Even Lyd's looking at me now. It was my mum who loved him and had a child with him but her emotions are shielded by her new family. I'm the one whose life this changes. He is my family, nothing to do with hers. Yet, if he is my family, I don't have a family. I only have Lyd, the baby growing inside her and my dead son.

"Don't worry about me," I finally manage to say. "I barely know the guy."

This brings tears to my mum's eyes. John nods with a gruff manly respect as though he thinks I'm only being strong for my mum. Chelsea stares at me like an alien. Lyd puts her hand on my shoulder. I have no idea why they're all so sorry for me.

When me and Lyd get to the hospice I ask the woman at reception whether we can visit Alan Watergate and she looks through a computer printout attached to a clipboard, tells us to hold on for a second and makes a phone call with a well-practiced inaudible voice.

After she hangs up she flicks her eyes across at us, smiles a tight-lipped smile and gets back to work on her computer. For the first ten seconds I think she might be doing something regarding us and then I realise that she's ignoring us. Just as I'm about to ask her for some information two nurses and a doctor, all female, approach. The doctor looks over at the receptionist, back at us and then back at her. The receptionist nods. The three of them approach us.

"Mr Watergate's son?" asks the doctor.

"Yes," I say, though I don't particularly agree with the terminology.

"I'm afraid your father passed away about an hour ago."

"Oh."

"I'm sorry."

"Thanks."

"Would you like to see him?"

I look at Lyd and at the two nurses, they all expect me to want to.

"Okay," I say.

"Follow me," says one of the nurses.

The doctor and the other nurse immediately branch off and head in another direction. I look back; Lyd's not coming with me. The look on her face reassures me that she thinks she's doing the right thing, that she has no right to see this dead man's body because she's never met him. The problem is that I don't particularly feel like I have the right either. I must have seen his living body less than ten times in my life.

After walking down a couple of squeaky-floored corridors I'm led into a room that has a plastic plaque inscribed, *Viewing Room*. It's just the same as the other rooms we passed on this corridor, with space for four patients, but in this room all four curtains are closed around the beds and there are no machines or extra pieces of furniture.

The nurse stands by the curtain. It crosses my mind that she might whip it open like a magician but she doesn't. She just stands there.

"Take as long as you need," she says, before walking away.

I find the gap in the curtain and step over to the bedside. The corpse looks like it had been very ill. Its cheeks are sunken and the skin yellowed with decay. Its eyes are closed and palms crossed neatly. He's not an old man. His hair is grey but he's not started balding. He looks a bit like me, or I look a bit like him. I don't feel much beyond a slight awkwardness. It's a shame he didn't get to see me, not that he deserved to.

I stare at him and try to think of feelings I might need to address. Loss isn't one. Abandonment almost touches a nerve but I pretty much got beyond that in my teenage years. Anger doesn't come, he's too dead. Denial is a possibility but I'm pretty sure I'm fully functioning and not repressing anything. Acceptance is the one and only feeling. It's simply happened. My father, who I never really knew, has died.

Rather than leaving the room at my first inclination I spend a couple of minutes standing over him, focusing on him, his body, his death. I force my mind back to him when it skips to Lyd, to the baby. I think about a time he turned up out of the blue when I was about six. I was shy and full of fear and wouldn't go near him. Mum grabbed me and put me on his knee out of charity. His breath smelt of sour coffee and ashtrays. The stink made me squeal and wriggle away from him, back to my toys. I remember his disappointed smile as he left. I glanced but didn't go to him. I had no idea who he was. I felt nothing. I feel nothing now. Perhaps the sadness of a missed opportunity. Perhaps not.

When I get back to Lyd she stands up and looks at me, desperately worried, pregnant, beautiful, alive.

"I'm fine. It was a bit weird but I'm fine."

"I'm sorry you didn't get to say goodbye," she says, hugging me.

"You don't miss what you never loved."

She laughs sadly and clings to me, and I hope that she's glad that I'm still here, still present.

Back at the house my mum is behaving manically because her first husband is dead and she can't figure out whether me and Lyd are back together and she doesn't dare ask. We're tired from the drive and, for a change, we would really welcome my family's usual sitting around and doing nothing philosophy but they're dressed for cold weather and there are no plans for dinner.

"It's Bonfire Night," says Chelsea, stopping herself from rolling her eyes in an act of sympathy.

I'd forgotten and my stomach sinks at the mention of it. I look at Lyd who is feeling similarly awkward. We always took Bonfire Night as our anniversary because we couldn't remember when we first made anything official.

Apparently, we have to go to Bitts Park for the *Fireshow*, eat pie and peas, hotdogs, toffee apples, burgers, candy floss, treacle toffee – "Whatever you want" – and watch the bonfire and fireworks display. I think about saying I'm not up for it but I've already implied that I'm fine. I look at Lyd and try to indicate with an expression that we could stay in if she's willing to blame her pregnancy for wanting to stay off her feet but she shrugs, unable to get my meaning, and we accept our fate.

"Sounds good," I say. "A bit of distraction."

We all pile into the car and head to Carlisle city centre. There are no parking spaces anywhere and some of the main through roads are closed. John knows how to manoeuvre around it all but we end up having to leave the car a ten-minute walk from Bitts Park (which makes Chelsea huff and grumble).

As we get closer, Chelsea keeps informing us that she can smell smoke so we must have missed the start of the bonfire and that we better not miss the start of the fireworks. Mum keeps calling her back, reminding her that Lyd is heavily pregnant. Random fireworks go off from people's back garden displays and each time my mum cringes slightly. I can't figure out if she's getting more nervous as she gets older or if she's so afraid of Chelsea's mood swings that she's flinching against the idea that the fireworks might have just started without us. Lyd suggests that they walk ahead but Mum says we'll never find each other if they do. John looks at his watch and assures us all that we'll make it in plenty of time.

The park is absolutely packed. I didn't know there were this many people in the whole of Cumbria. John informs me that thirty-five thousand people were expected. The crowd has turned all of the grass underfoot into muddy sludge. Most people (including my mum, Chelsea and John) are wearing wellies. Me and Lyd, unprepared, are wearing normal, not particularly waterproof shoes.

Embers and flakes of carbon are wafting by more and more frequently. Noise from a couple of fairground rides and a number of pounding speakers mixes with the general hubbub of the crowd. As we finally see the enormous bonfire, Chelsea speedily breaks away from us.

"Where are you going?" calls Mum.

"To meet Becca."

"Have you got money?"

"Yeah."

"Where will we see you?"

"I've got my mobile."

Chelsea disappears into the crowd.

"That's why her knickers were in a twist," says Mum. "She didn't want to miss her mates."

The bonfire has been made out of pallets, nailed together in a pyramid structure about twenty feet high. The wood is quick burning and there are lots of gaps for air so the flame is tall, sweeping and yellow, rising ten feet above the structure. The sides are already beginning to collapse inwards even though it must have been lit less than twenty minutes ago.

All the way around the fire, about ten feet from its edge, is a seven-foot anti-climb metal barrier fence. It's see-through, for the most part, but the best view of the bonfire seems to be in a region where its heat is ineffectual. We find a sweet spot on a raised bit of ground where we can see the fire over the fence and just about feel the heat.

I have a memory of being here as a child, standing extremely close to the naked flame of a bonfire made of logs, wooden cabinets, shelves and old couches, poisonous green flames rising from seat covers, sticky toffee all over my burning cheeks, forgetting I was with anyone, looking at the fire until my eyes were so dry that I couldn't blink. Was I with my dad?

The bonfire crackles and pops loudly, bringing me out of my daydream. Thousands of tiny cinders fizz up into the sky. About a fifth of the crowd releases a vowel noise. Mum tells us to wait where we are whilst she and John get us all pie and peas. When Lyd says she doesn't want meat, Mum represses a mini-meltdown and says she'll do the best she can.

When they're gone I put my arm around Lyd's waist. She takes a step away, puts her hand on her stomach and looks at me.

"It's still not right," she says.

"You and me?"

"The bump."

"They always say pregnancy's different every time."

"Not this different. I can't feel the shape of it. And when it kicks, it doesn't feel right. I can't explain it."

"So it's not a big kicker."

"Knock on my stomach."

"I'm not going to knock on our baby."

"Well, just feel it then."

I put my hand on her stomach. It's incredibly firm and solid.

"Sometimes you see women who look like they've got a beach ball inside them," I say. "I think it's a good sign that you're so big and firm."

"I've had weird cravings. Mud. Twigs. I wanted to eat worms last week. I'm constantly exhausted. It feels like something really weird is happening in there."

"The sonographer said everything was fine."

"I know."

"We could probably arrange another ultrasound, even now?"

"Maybe I'm just a bit delirious. I can't believe how tired I am. I was still working when my water broke last time."

"And five minutes after it broke."

She smiles.

"Don't take this the wrong way," I say, "but you were six years younger then. That's a long time on the biological clock."

"I know. Maybe I'm just getting old, and paranoid."

"It's completely understandable."

"Is it?"

"Of course. It's precarious, giving birth. Dangerous. It must be scary seeing a bump that big and knowing that it's got to come out of you."

"I guess so. I just wanted everything to be right by now. If it wasn't for this…"

"What?"

"Nothing. We shouldn't be talking about me. You've just lost your dad."

"I want to talk about you."

"You're dealing with it so well. I think you really might be back to your old self, better than your old self."

"I know you think I'm being brave but I'm not. I feel like I came to Carlisle to see a stranger's dead body. And I know it's my dad and that should make me feel something, but it doesn't. If anything, it's made me realise that John's the closest thing I've got to a dad. I didn't have a father. You know? It felt like a bit of a shame, like there were things I'd never know, but mostly it was just a dead guy."

Lyd looks at me. I look at the bonfire.

"Vince, I don't want you to think it's more than it is, but I'm going to move back in. I'm not saying we're getting back together. I just think it's time I came back."

I'm about to respond when Mum and John arrive with four portions of pie and peas. Mum's frantically excited because they had cheese-and-onion pies so Lyd doesn't have to miss out. The rest of us have steak, which is actually mincemeat. The pastry is rubbery and the filling is sparse but I'm unexpectedly famished now that I'm holding something warm. I eat quickly and keep glancing at Lyd.

A local radio DJ is announcing the countdown to "the best fireworks show in the North" on a stage that we can't see on the opposite side of the bonfire. The heat from the thirty-foot mound of flame has dried my face. My cheeks are taut. After the countdown there is a desolate four seconds where thirty-five thousand people quietly look up at an empty black sky.

When the fireworks begin squealing their way up into the air I look at Lyd as she watches the explosions. Her face is incomparable with the one I first saw on Bonfire Night nearly eight years ago. Now, after her love for Charlie, the worry that came with it, and her loss, the grief of it all, and with this new child inside her, exhausting her, her face has been robbed of its scientific appreciation for coloured gunpowder exploding in the sky. In its place is the face of a strong woman, a mother, someone who has seen beyond herself, loved and lost something so powerfully that it has destroyed her but also shown her how to rebuild a life from rubble. She is full of the wisdom of experience and, whether she knows it or not, she is going to be an excellent mother. Those first-child temptations are gone: the need to spoil, to over-love, to imagine everything is perfect and will go on being perfect forever. In their place an emotional realism has taken hold, an affinity with the struggle of life. There will be no pretence, no over-happy fixation. This child will see the lines in its mother's face and gradually intuit the pain that love can cause, the complexity of emotions that life can instil, and it will walk into the wider world a little bit more prepared because of it.

Lyd glances at me.

"You're supposed to be looking up there," she says.

"Are you really coming home?"

She nods but there is a warning in her eyes, *Don't let one thing mean another*. I nod back and put my arm around her waist. She lets me keep it there. I catch my mum glancing and smiling, nudging John (who can't figure out that she wants him to look at us). I look up. A group of red fireworks fill the sky.

"That's lithium," says Lyd. "The red ones have lithium in them."

"Is it?" I say, trying to cling to my hopes.

FIVE

In physics, a singularity is a theoretical space at the centre of a black hole with zero volume and infinite density. In mechanics, a singularity occurs when a system or machine reaches a position or configuration where the subsequent behaviour cannot be predicted. In mathematics, a singularity is the point at which a mathematical set fails to be "well-behaved". In all these cases, there is a singular point of incomprehension, where logic undoes itself and change is absolute. It goes against everything that has come before, yet somehow epitomises it.

Lyd waddles down the stairs behind me, reading my book. I have a letter in the morning post. It's official-looking and I'm anxious about receiving demands for the thousands of pounds I owe my ex-publisher. One of the terms set out in the big relationship talk me and Lyd had is that the publisher's debt is my problem. There will be no financial bailout.

I've spent the last few weeks morosely contemplating my options. English teacher? Can't afford the course fees. A profession? Can't afford the training. Set up my own little printing press? Can't afford the start-up costs. Any job, anywhere? Don't have the experience. I've been thinking about setting up a creative writing course in a night school somewhere but it's been looking more and more like I'm going to have to swallow my pride and find something menial and unskilled so that I can pay off my debts.

I open the letter and read it as I make my way to the kitchen.

"What is it?" asks Lyd, looking up from the A4 pages, noticing the consternation on my face.

"I don't believe it."

"What?"

"My dad left me some money. Whatever's left after the house is sold and the debts are paid off."

"Will there be much?"

"They're predicting about eighteen thousand."

"That's—"

"Enough to pay off the publisher."

"And buy the final stock."

"Do you think I should bother?"

"You can sell them at readings when this one comes out."

"*If* it comes out."

"I can't put it down."

"You have to say that."

"I do and I don't. I don't have to say it like that. There's something about these last few chapters especially."

"Where are you?"

"The last chapter, I think. It's all coming together really well."

"I had this creative surge. I wrote the last five chapters in about two weeks."

"It's the best writing you've ever done."

"I'm worried what you'll think about the ending."

"There's not all that much that could go wrong at this stage."

"Just wait," I say.

"Eighteen thousand?"

"I know. It never occurred to me that he might leave me money. I suppose I presumed he didn't have any."

"It's about time you had a bit of good fortune."

"Maybe I should spend it on teacher training?"

"You've spent the last fifteen years learning your profession. You're a writer, not a teacher."

"I know. But writing's not really a profession anymore."

"It is for some people."

"Not many."

"Everything seemed more problematic before I read this. Let's just see how it lands."

I kiss her neck just behind the ear.

"Stop building my hopes up," I say.

"What? It's good. But leave me alone," she says. "I want to finish it."

"You can't. We've got to go and meet Serge and Gloria."

"But it will only take about quarter of an hour."

"We promised. I think they're trying to make an effort to get back on track with things."

"Okay. But I'm taking it with me. I'll finish it on the way."

"I'm feeling very bolstered by all this praise."

She smirks.

"Well, don't be. Everybody else might hate it."

Walking down Archway Road towards the café that does the fancy bread, Italian fillings and decent coffee, I'm looking over Lyd's shoulder, reading the last chapter with her. She's just coming up to the last four pages and my stomach is turning.

"I want you to stop now. I don't want you to read the end. It's too weird."

"Shh. Leave me alone. You're ruining it."

"Sorry."

"Get away. Let me read it."

"Okay. Okay."

I pull away from her and smile to myself. Her interest in my work makes me feel whole. Whatever I write, she's my chosen audience. Her heart has the only ear I want to whisper into. As long as she responds to my words, thinks they're good work and were worth writing, then it doesn't matter so much what the rest of the world thinks.

My ears pop and start ringing.

As my hearing comes back it dawns on me that there's birdsong everywhere, blackbird song. I look up and see hundreds of black males on the rooftops, orchestras of yellow beaks. At this time of year most of the blackbirds in London have migrated to Cornwall for the milder air. And blackbirds don't gather like this. They occasionally play together in spring but they're too territorial to perch besides each other or fly together. This type of clustering, particularly at this time of year, is unheard of. The sight of all the black feathers and the sound of all the whistling is making me feel light-headed. Nobody else on the street seems to have noticed them.

"Have you seen all the—"

I turn to Lyd but she's no longer by my side. I look around, panicking. The birdsong is so loud that I can't hear anything else. I finally catch sight of her. She's so engrossed in the last few pages of my novel that she hasn't registered a kink in the road. She's veering away from me. She doesn't stop or look up where I expect her to. She takes an extra step and her foot twists on the edge of the kerb, forcing her to take three quick steps so that she doesn't fall down onto her stomach. She's suddenly standing in the middle of the road, confused, holding three hundred pieces of A4 paper. There is a screeching sound. A black van with a yellow trim is sliding along the road. Lyd doesn't have time.

"Baby!" I cry, reaching a hand forward, watching helplessly.

The van slams into Lyd's pregnant stomach, knocking her a metre through the air and onto the floor, coming to a squealing stop with its bumper above her knees. Hundreds of blackbirds fly up into the air. Small wings flap in a million different directions, chaotically wafting me around as I move towards her, as she clutches her stomach, cries with pain.

I can see blood on her face, on her hands. Pages of my novel scatter in the wind. Familiar words blow past my eyes. My brain feels high up. My body is toppling. As I get close to her I stumble, somehow spinning one hundred and eighty degrees, but I just manage to save myself from falling. I spin one hundred and eighty degrees back towards her but my legs are giving in, I'm sinking, scratching at the blackness, trying to get back to my mind so I can help, but the inward pull is too great. I'm gone before I hit the ground.

I wake up in an ambulance.

"Where is she?" I ask, trying to sit up with a paramedic's hand restraining me.

"She's here," he says. "Look. Right there."

I look across to the other side of the ambulance. Lyd is on the main medical bed. I'm on a foldout thing that has been pulled down from the wall.

"Lyd? *Lyd*? What's going on? Why can't she hear me?"

"She's unconscious," says the paramedic.

"The baby?"

"We're not sure," he says.

"What do you mean you're not sure?"

"There seems to be some kind of anomaly," he says.

My stomach turns.

"Is there a heartbeat? Is it alive?"

I try to sit up and he attempts to restrain me again but I catch a glimpse of blood between Lyd's legs and rip him away from me. A confused medic is moving his stethoscope around on her pregnant stomach which now looks like a rocky mountainscape. Mucus-thick red blood covers her crotch area and is drooling down from the bed onto the floor of the ambulance.

"What the hell is going on?" I wail. "What are you doing? Why aren't you saving her?"

"We don't know what we're dealing with," says the paramedic.

"You're dealing with a pregnant woman who got hit by a van!"

"No," he says, very certain and very sternly, "we're not."

227

When we get to the hospital everything becomes a blur. No matter how much I struggle, they won't let me go with Lyd. They take me to a waiting room where I rock back and forth on an uncomfortable chair. They make me sign things that seem completely irrelevant.

Finally, they tell me she's prepped for an emergency operation that might or might not be a caesarean section and that if I really want to, and they advise against it, there's an observation window I can watch from.

I go with them.

A surgeon makes a long, deep incision in Lyd's bumpy abdomen. His hands are quick. I close my eyes for a moment. The surgeon makes lots of precise adjustments to the incision and cuts away some fatty tissue whilst a male nurse dabs at the blood. When the surgeon makes a vertical cut into Lyd's womb, a litre of thick red albumen pours out of her. The surgeon recoils and looks at his colleagues, confused, asking for advice. The viscous red gloop pours over her hips and between her legs, off the sides of the operating table and onto the floor. One of the nurses runs out of the theatre and comes back with a bucket and mop.

After a little debate the surgeon goes in with some forceps and pulls out a shard of something bluish white. He does this again and again, pulling more and more strange white shards out of her, dropping them into a metal tray. His brow is knitting tighter and tighter. Though the pressure has eased, the red albumen keeps oozing. The nurse mopping the floor just seems to be spreading the thick red slime around.

After five or ten minutes pulling out increasingly smaller white shards from Lyd's womb, the surgeon seems satisfied and goes in deeper with the forceps. All the people around the operating table lean in to see.

The thing he pulls out has big, fuzzy purple bulbs on top of its head and a yellowish fleshy flap instead of a face. Its arms are hooked over, webbed, speckled with what look like wet black feathers. One male nurse runs to a bin to vomit, another nurse holds her hand to the patch over her mouth. Two doctors take the creature to a separate table whilst the surgeon begins to take more white shards out of Lyd.

I don't know where to look. There is too much thick red albumen. It's everywhere. It covers every apron, it's on every bare arm, it almost covers the floor. Over by the creature two doctors are scratching their heads, looking really closely at the centre of it. They seem to have come to some sort of agreement. They bend over it with medical tools I can't decipher the functions of. I can't see what they're doing.

On the main table a nurse is vacuuming Lyd's insides and the surgeon is shining a light into her womb. The two nurses holding the wound open are looking away, squeezing their eyes closed. The gurgling sound the suction device makes inside her is making me queasy, even though the sound is muffled by the glass.

Back on the small table the two doctors put something that looks like a large orange turkey wing with tufts of black feathers into a metal tray. They look at each other and nod, leaning back in. Thirty seconds later another raw, limp turkey wing is put in the metal tray. Now, they both move in very close and work very carefully.

The gurgling stops.

Over on the operating table they expertly sew Lyd's womb, tissue and skin back together.

One of the two doctors over with the creature puts a long yellow flap and a cap of skin with two furry purple bulbs into the metal tray. Both doctors look at each other with amazement, carefully pull some loose strips of skin away and put them in the metal tray, and then pass something small and purple to one of the nurses. She goes to wash it in a sink.

Lyd's wound has been dressed. I can see the machines she's attached to and nothing is flashing or making irregular noises.

A nurse comes towards the door to the viewing room with something wrapped in a small green sheet. As she approaches everybody in the room gathers around her. In the doorway she doesn't say a word. None of them do. When she passes it to me I don't expect to see what I do. It's a baby. I look up at them all. They are all peering down.

"What is it?" I ask.

All of them are silent. I have to open the blanket and find out for myself.

It's a girl.

I wrap her back up and bob her up and down. Relief gushes through me, tears and joy and confusion. She's so light and precious.

"I don't understand," I say.

Nobody responds.

"*I don't understand.*"

One of the two doctors who put the hooked wings and yellow flap into the metal tray steps towards me.

"Neither do we," he says. "They should both be dead. But it looks like they're both going to make it."

I look down at our little girl's face. She is still immersed in non-being but signals are beginning to prod at her: light on her translucent eyelids, new temperatures, the emptiness of air compared to liquid, the coarseness of cotton over flesh, weight and gravity, disconnection. It's too early for her to grasp any of this but her brow wrinkles. An ancient black secret escapes her. She pulls back towards nothingness but life has her. She is slowly coming into being, stuck here. She cries. She wants to go back, where all the secrets and miracles hide.

SIX

I am the forgotten connections, the untold stories, the lost sensations, the useless facts. If somebody needs to hear a song, I sing it. If somebody needs to see a sign, I show it. I had never saved a soul. I had never touched the truth. I was no more than a thing that said I...

"Vince."

I'm sitting on the couch holding my fountain pen with a plain black notebook resting on my thigh. It's open on the first page, blank. Lyd is nursing Merula beside me.

"Huh?"

"You were miles away."

"I was thinking about when we were first getting together." I chuckle.

"What's so funny?"

"You were always talking about string theory. Constantly."

"So what?" she says, smiling.

"At first, everything that came out your mouth was completely baffling but then, after about the third time we met, you started dumbing it down for me."

"Ohhh, that must have been when I realised you were an idiot."

"Around then, yes. I remember you said that everything in the universe might be made of these tiny strings, and if it was, all space, all matter, light, gravity, everything, when you looked really close, would look similar to sound waves. And what made one thing a rock and another thing a sunbeam was just the way it vibrated. Everything was made of the same thing. It was all just vibrations travelling through vibrations, like a giant symphony."

"It seems so long since I've had the time to think like that. I've been so entrenched in the details."

"That's when I knew how successful you were going to be. I knew if you could get me to understand it you could get anyone to."

"I think those chats were the preamble to writing my book," she says.

"I'm glad I could help."

"I've actually been thinking about writing another."

"That's great. What about?"

"Probably supersymmetry. It seems like the right time."

"Definitely."

Merula stops nursing and milk drools down her chin. Lyd wipes it away gently with her thumb and tucks her breast away. I lean over and give Merula a kiss on the cheek.

"I think it might be a while before I can write anything again," I say.

"You deserve a break. You wrote a novel in nine months. That's quicker than usual isn't it?"

"I guess."

"You can't just bounce from one thing to the next."

I look at her, supporting Merula's little head, close the notebook and move closer to them.

"I just don't like being at a loose end," I say. "I need a project to be getting on with."

"I've got an eighteen-year project for you right here."

I take Merula whilst she buttons up her shirt.

"I know," I say. "But it's not the same."

"It'll come. Don't worry. Did Angela get back to you yet?"

"Not yet. She said she'd put it to the top of the slush pile. If I don't hear anything within a couple of weeks I'll start putting in the administrative grind, try and get it into the right hands."

"And in the meanwhile?"

"Just keep following my nose."

"You'll think of something."

"The words always find me in the end."

"Exactly."

Jamal opens his door and stands aside for me to enter his front room. The floor is covered with pieces of scrap metal and motor parts on newspapers. It's just as crowded and inhospitable as it used to be.

"I see you've taken up your old habits again."

"Not all of them," he says, shutting the front door.

"Just the worst ones?"

"A man who starts again usually chooses the same path."

"Are you going all Zen master on me already? How many joints did you smoke this morning?"

"Shut up. Let me show you something."

"Here," I say, handing him a print-out of my book. "Take this first."

"Great, thanks, man. I'll get started on it later."

He puts it down on top of a car battery on the coffee table and heads up the stairs (each of which has a carburettor pushed to the right-hand side on top of a newspaper).

At the doorway of his workshop, after looking into the room for a couple of seconds, he turns and looks my way.

"Isn't it beautiful?"

I approach him and look through the doorway. He's built an entire Rolls Royce in his workshop. But it is no longer a workshop. All the shelves have been taken down and all the tools are gone from the back wall. The walls have been painted white and the room is lit like a car showroom. His black Silver Shadow is gleaming. It looks like it just rolled off the assembly line.

I start laughing.

"You're crazy," I say.

He walks around the side, opens one of the bedroom windows (which were previously covered by the hardboard wall of tools), feeds out a hose pipe connected to the car's exhaust pipe and closes his new thick black curtains. He then reaches up and clicks the side of a big box that is hanging from the ceiling, a projector.

"Turn the lights off," he says, grinning.

As I do this he sits in the driver's seat. A bright blue rectangle is projected across two of the walls and then replaced by the image of his desktop (I didn't know he even owned a computer). He rolls down the passenger window.

"Come on," he says. "You're riding shotgun."

I shake my head with a smile and get into the car.

"Only you would build a beautiful car in your spare bedroom. What's the point if you can't drive it?"

"Who says I can't drive it?" he says, starting the engine.

The machine hums and vibrates at a smooth, even level.

"We're not going to die of carbon-monoxide poisoning, are we?"

"You just saw me put the pipe out the window."

"Still…"

"I'm alive, aren't I?"

"Sort of," I say, with a smirk.

"Quiet a second," he says, indicating with a hand to his ear that I should be listening to the engine. "Isn't it beautiful? I could listen to that sound forever."

"It definitely sounds like a car."

"Come off it," he says, squeezing the accelerator. "Tell me that's not beautiful."

"It sounds great," I admit. "I don't think you'll get very far though."

I gesture towards the walls in every direction.

"There's all these videos you can download. They're amazing. I've cruised down Route 66, put in sixty laps at Silverstone, I even did the Rally de Portugal. I felt a bit sick after that one."

I'm laughing.

"There are these great railway ones too," he continues. "I know it's a bit weird, sitting in a car, but I did a four-and-a-half-hour trip from Glasgow to Mallaig last week. It goes over Fort William. Such a lovely journey."

"You have taken recluse to a whole new level."

"Who needs to leave the house when you have this? I never thought I'd get into the Internet, any of this technological stuff, but, you'll see. I'm going to do the Trans-Siberian Railway at some point. I've got the full six days of footage. And there's Big Sur, Nurburgring Nordschleife, Ruta 40, Conor Pass, Karakoram Highway, so many great drives. And people are just giving these videos away. I couldn't afford to do all these trips in real life even if I wanted to."

"I have to hand it to you," I say, "you have assimilated into your suburban isolation with a great sense of adventure."

"I got one especially for you."

"Ominous."

"Not at all," he says, beginning to click though folders. "Here it is."

"How have you got the screen so big?" I ask. "It's in the side windows."

"Just a bit of keystoning. It's a decent projector. It's got two heads."

"Look at you, part of the twenty-first century."

"Shush, just feel the engine vibrating through your feet and watch."

"Aye, aye, Captain."

The room goes black. It's immediately apparent that he has the car wired up for sound, very good quality sound.

The room lights up.

We're in the desert, with rocky mountains on the horizon and scaffolding in the foreground. A hissing noise slowly builds and builds until it explodes into a roar. The Rolls Royce shakes with the bass of it, the engine gently purring beneath. The scaffolding falls away. The camera spins slowly and we begin to rocket upwards. The huge mountain range quickly begins to look flat. Everything rumbles and vibrates. We pass a layer of small intermittent clouds. The desert below looks fuzzy from the heat. The roar goes on.

Long thin strips of white cloud slowly sink around us. The desert and the mountains shrink and shrivel. Over half of the view is blue sky. The sun makes me squint as it passes across the windscreen. For a couple of seconds everything beneath us is a mixture of vapours that the eye can't see through but then a misty cloud falls away, revealing the surface below.

The roar thunders on. The flat horizon begins to curve. The desert is now just a small portion of the Earth which is mostly ocean. The sky's upper horizon starts bending, shifting through all the deepest blues until there is an encroaching curve of blackness. This blackness pulls down, further and further, until the portion of blue that accounts for the sky is a thin, ethereal blue ribbon wrapped around a blue and white marble floating in nothingness.

A bright white light, a spotlight that used to be the yellow sun, with a centre that the camera cannot interpret as anything other than its brightest and whitest pixels, crosses the blackness as our rocket rotates, travelling diagonally, looking for nothing. The roaring of the scorched fuel settles into brassy reverberations. A booster pack is released and slowly floats backwards.

My stomach lifts.

The sound is dead.

We're suspended in the vast blackness of space, spinning slowly, almost unnoticeably. The stars begin to multiply. The darkness between them deepens. It crosses my mind that, before the universe, there was an endless black hole, an infinite singularity, and that our universe is expanding into it. Our black holes are bubbles of that spaceless and timeless truth beyond us: death. And this death should not be feared as an evil, decimating force. It is formless and eternal, complete and inconceivable; part of a truth we cannot measure or judge.

Floating in an imaginary vacuum, suspended in disbelief, I get the sensation that the universe is expanding. This death beyond the stars is in retreat. I've almost forgotten that I'm sitting in a stationary Rolls Royce in a bedroom in Highgate. I don't hear the rumble of the engine, the hum of the projector, the pause in my breath. The camera spins slowly. The world is edging back into view.

COME AND VISIT US AT
WWW.LEGENDPRESS.CO.UK

FOLLOW US @LEGEND_PRESS